# Nobody's
# Orphan

*Other Avon Camelot Books by*
**Anne Lindbergh**

THE HUNKY-DORY DAIRY

ANNE LINDBERGH can hardly remember *not* writing. Born in New York City, she grew up in Connecticut in a house filled with books. Since her parents—Anne Morrow Lindbergh and Charles A. Lindbergh—were both writers, she was encouraged in her own writing of poems and stories, which she began at an early age.

Anne Lindbergh lived in Paris off and on for fifteen years and now lives in McLean, Virginia. She is the author of several popular books for young readers, including *The Hunky-Dory Dairy,* an Avon Camelot book.

# Nobody's Orphan

## Anne Lindbergh

AN AVON CAMELOT BOOK

There is no Saint Michael's Church in Georgetown. Both the church and Martha's after-school group are figments of the author's imagination.

Excerpts from the poems by Robert Service are reprinted from *The Collected Poems of Robert Service* by permission of Dodd, Mead & Company, Inc.; McGraw-Hill Ryerson Limited; and Ernest Benn, Ltd.

AVON BOOKS
A division of
The Hearst Corporation
105 Madison Avenue
New York, New York 10016

Copyright © 1983 by Anne Lindbergh
Published by arrangement with Harcourt Brace Jovanovich, Publishers
Library of Congress Catalog Card Number: 83-8499
ISBN: 0-380-70395-5
RL: 5.3

The Harcourt Brace Jovanovich edition contains the following Library of Congress Cataloging in Publication Data:

Lindbergh, Anne.
  Nobody's orphan.

  Summary: Martha, the only green-eyed member of a brown-eyed family, is convinced she is adopted, but thinks she wouldn't mind it so much, if only her parents would let her have a dog.
  [1. Family life—Fiction. 2. Dogs—Fiction. 3. Adoption—Fiction] I. Title.
PZ7.L6572 No      1982      [Fic]      83-8499

First Camelot Printing: December 1987

CAMELOT TRADEMARK REG. U.S. PAT. OFF. AND IN OTHER COUNTRIES, MARCA REGISTRADA, HECHO EN U.S.A.

Printed in the U.S.A.

OPM 10 9 8 7 6 5 4 3 2 1

FOR MY DAUGHTER CONSTANCE

*"Thoughts into my head do come
Thick as flies upon a plum."*

—EDWARD LEAR

# Nobody's Orphan

# Chapter 1

I might as well tell you two things right away: my name is Martha, and I have green eyes. I'm not proud of either of those facts, but they're important because they're what first convinced me that I was an orphan.

Both my parents have brown eyes, and so does my brother Kermit. If that isn't a clue, I'd like to know what is! Besides, nobody in my family has ever been called a stupid name like Martha. Why Martha?

"We like the name," my mother kept saying.

I didn't believe her for a minute. She just said that to make me feel better. For my tenth birthday she gave me a gold chain with "Martha" hanging from it in six separate gold letters. She also gave me a pair of shoelaces that said "Martha" twenty-two times on each lace. The necklace was nice, but I never wore the laces. They were too embarrassing. I told my parents that the least they could have done was change my name after they got me from the adoption agency. They just laughed.

"Why are you so anxious to become an orphan?" my father asked.

What a dumb question! In books and movies, all the best things happen to orphans. Look at Annie and how she ends up in a mansion with a dog of her own! I could do without the mansion, but I was dying for a dog.

"Don't you think we're a happy family?" my father asked.

"Of course I do!" I told him. "I love you more than my real parents. If my real parents turned up now, I wouldn't even know them! I just want to get the records straight."

"*We're* your real parents," my father kept saying patiently. That is, he thought he was being patient with me. Actually I was being patient with him.

"If you were my real parents, you'd care more about my feelings," I said. "If I can't change my name, couldn't I at least have a dog?"

I had been wanting a dog for a long time. Probably my whole life, as a matter of fact, because I can't remember a time when I ever *didn't* want a dog. But my parents always said no because we traveled around too much. They said no this time too.

"If I had a dog, I wouldn't mind so much about being an orphan," I argued.

"You're too old for fairy tales," said my father. "We've been through all this before. I refuse to discuss it."

The reason we traveled around so much is that my father is in the Foreign Service, so my brother Kermit and I have spent most of our lives in foreign countries.

Now, there's another crazy name: Kermit! I kept telling Kermit he was an orphan too, but Kermit just said he didn't want to be an orphan, and he liked his name. Whatever I said that year, he would say just the opposite. He still does.

As a matter of fact, I was pretty sure that Kermit was my parents' real child. There were plenty of photographs of him as a tiny baby, and even one of my mother pregnant with him, standing in front of the Eiffel Tower. I'm in that one too, squinting and holding a pink balloon. It was my third birthday. But there were no photos of me at all until I was over two years old. Now, if that wasn't a clue, what was? My father said that my baby pictures were all in a suitcase that got lost when we were moving from Brussels to Paris, but I didn't believe him for a minute.

In any case, we weren't living in foreign countries when all this happened. We had just moved to Washington, D.C., and Kermit and I were going to public school right in our neighborhood, which was Georgetown.

At first I thought it was going to be a great year. The private schools I went to abroad were really hard, especially in math, which is not my best subject. I had the idea that public schools were easy and maybe didn't teach math at all.

Another thing I was looking forward to was horseback riding. My parents weren't about to give in about getting a dog, but to make me feel better, they said I could learn to ride. I hate sports but I love animals, so I was pretty excited about the idea.

I joined the fourth-grade class in January, and Kermit went into first. He was crazy about his teacher and got along really well with the kids. My teacher was all right, but the kids were horrible, and the worst of them all was a girl called Parker.

Parker threw wet paper towels at me in the girls' room, she hid my Spanish folder, and she borrowed my pen without asking and lost it. It was the pen my father got at the White House, and I had a lot of trouble about it because I happened to have borrowed it from my father without asking.

When I mentioned it to Parker, she told everybody I was showing off, and they all started calling me "Hothead," which I know for a fact was Parker's idea, even though now she swears it wasn't. But that's because now she's my best friend.

Parker's whole name is Bettysue Parker Ames. I found that out from the school directory. What happened is that it turned out they taught math in public schools, the same as anywhere else, and I was still terrible at it. I kept forgetting to copy down my assignment, and one day my mother got fed up. She said she wasn't going to accept any excuses. I had to call up a friend in my class and ask what the math homework was.

I said I didn't have any friends in my class. This was just after the Hothead incident. So my mother got out the directory, and right away she asked, "What about Bettysue Ames?"

"There isn't any Bettysue Ames," I told her. "There's just Parker Ames."

"Bettysue Parker Ames," my mother read. "Here's her name, printed right under yours. See for yourself."

I looked over her shoulder and saw that she was right. "Martha Albright, Bettysue Parker Ames, Peter

Brodsky," the directory read, and then it went on through the alphabet.

That was how I found out that Parker's first name was Bettysue, and I took advantage of it. I know it was a mean trick because I understand how people feel about names. If I had a middle name, I would use it instead of Martha. But I didn't have one.

So the next day I took Parker aside during recess and said, "Listen, Bettysue, if you don't stop calling me Hothead, the whole school will be calling you Bettysue by this time tomorrow. And don't say it wasn't your fault because I won't believe you."

Well, Parker is no chicken. She doesn't like being pushed around, and now that we are best friends, I really respect her for it. She took a swing at me with her lunchbox, and I tripped her and pinned her down on the playground. A lot of other kids came over to watch, and a teacher sent us both to the office. The principal happened to be out to lunch. We got so bored waiting for her that before we knew it, we were friends.

The rest of my year in fourth grade was great, especially since it turned out that I loved riding. My father knew some people with a farm in Virginia, and they let us use two of their horses. My father and I went out there every Sunday, just the two of us because my mother and Kermit weren't interested. We would ride all afternoon and then stop for ice cream on the way home. Life was just about perfect. Then suddenly everything went wrong at once.

First of all, Parker came over one day at the end of August and told me her parents were sending her to a private school.

I couldn't believe it. We had been best friends since March. We sat at the same desk at school. We didn't even bother to separate our Magic Markers because we really trusted each other. On weekends if Parker didn't spend the night with me, I spent the night with her. When Parker's cat had seven kittens, she gave me six and kept only one for herself. Until my parents found out, that is. They made her take them back.

Then we went to day camp together all summer, and when camp was over, we made a clubhouse in a kind of shed for trash cans that nobody was using in the back alley. We had lots of plans for fifth grade, so you can imagine my surprise.

"What happened?" I asked. "Did they flunk you out of public school?"

"They never flunk you; they just make you repeat," said Parker. "If it happened to anyone, it would happen to you. It probably will, as soon as they find out you never learned your sevens tables."

This was a sore spot, but I didn't mind as much hearing it from Parker. "Was it a behavior problem?" I asked, changing the subject.

Parker didn't even answer. She was on the traffic squad, and she always got A's in citizenship. As a matter of fact, she got A's in math too.

"I don't know what happened," she said. "My parents always said they'd send me to private school, and they finally got around to doing it. I can't bike to school anymore. I have to get picked up in a dumb old school bus. I don't get home until four-thirty, and I have to wear a uniform. It's horrible!"

For a minute after she told me, I tried to remember

the other kids in our class. I couldn't think of a single name. Going back without Parker would be like starting out all over again in a new school.

Then gradually the names came back to me, along with a couple of faces. I had this mental picture of Peter Brodsky and Scott Fratelli and Gloria Vasquez, and I knew it was going to be a bad year.

To make things worse, I found a terrific stray dog, and right away my parents said I couldn't keep him. He was a scruffy black Lab with just a red bandana tied around his neck, no collar or tags or anything. He followed me home the last Sunday in August when I was out buying the paper with Kermit. It was obvious he hadn't had a meal for weeks, so we brought him inside and fed him.

We named him Ronald Reagan, and Kermit and I took turns having him sleep in our beds at night. My mother kept reminding us that we had to find Ronald's owner, but my father happened to be away just then, and she kind of let things slide.

My father had been to South America, and his flight got delayed three times on the way back, so he wasn't in such a good mood. At first it wasn't too bad because Parker was there, and he thought Ronald Reagan belonged to Parker. My father is usually so polite to Parker that sometimes I wonder if he isn't joking.

"Any friend of Parker's is a friend of mine," he said when I introduced Ronald, but he didn't look as if he meant it.

"Thank you, Mr. Albright," said Parker. "It took a while before Ronald would make friends with me, though. Martha is his favorite because she fed him four pounds of ground round. And he likes Kermit best at night because Kermit's bed stinks."

I could have killed her! My bed smells just as good as Kermit's bed, and it's much more comfortable for Ronald because I don't sleep with eight locomotives. But the point is that my father threw a fit. He told my mother to get him three aspirins and a bottle of club water, and when she came back, he told her to take away the aspirins and bring some Scotch instead. Then he said he refused to have Ronald in the house.

Parker snuck away when she saw how things were going, so she wasn't any help, but Kermit was more cooperative than I ever would have expected. Instead of screaming and calling my father names, he turned white as a sheet and threw up on the kitchen floor. Then he went to bed, even though it was only six P.M.

You have no idea how effective throwing up can be. My father gave in and let Ronald sleep in Kermit's room that night. It was my turn, but I didn't say anything because I was so grateful. But my father said we had to put signs all over the neighborhood saying we had found a lost dog, and as soon as Ronald's owner turned up, Ronald had to go.

When I printed the sign the next day, I tried to make Ronald as hard to recognize as possible.

"Are you sure the name is Ronald Reagan?" my father asked when he saw it. "That mutt is a female!"

So I had to take out the name and just write: "Female Black Labrador Retriever" instead. I tried "Black Mutt," but I didn't get away with it.

My father photocopied the sign at his office, and after he got home, I put thirty copies up on neighborhood trees. But Parker knew about it, and she went around on her bike and took them all down again. So Ronald stayed on as our guest, and she was a pretty good guest, except for one thing.

I woke up on the first day of school with this terrible rash all over me. Actually I didn't notice it right away because I was in such a hurry to get to school on time, but the other fifth-graders picked it up the minute I walked into the classroom.

"Hey, look at Hothead!" Gloria yelled. "She's got the measles!"

I hoped it *was* measles, but it turned out to be fleas. My mother got out the phone book and looked up the number of the dog pound. I think she really would have called it, too, if something hadn't happened that took her mind off Ronald.

My father came home from work early that day. He and my mother shut themselves up in the living room and talked until I banged on the door and said it was late for supper. It wasn't until after supper that Kermit and I found out what it was all about. My father told us to stay at the table because he had something to tell us, and I could see by his face that it was something pretty serious.

"What's up?" I asked. "There's no use trying to keep it a secret."

My father smiled, but he didn't look very happy. My mother looked as if she had a headache.

"It isn't a secret, Martha," my father said, "but it's not a happy surprise for any of us."

"Your father isn't working in Washington after all this winter," my mother explained. "The government is sending him to South America instead."

"Terrific!" I yelled. "I bet they don't teach math in South America!" Then I stamped around a little and shouted "Olé!" but nobody thought it was funny.

"I'm sorry to disappoint you, Martha," my father continued, "but it's not going to be a family project this time. I'll be home sometime in the spring. Meanwhile, you and your mother and Kermit will go on living here."

I couldn't stand it. First Parker changing schools, then finding a stray dog that I wasn't allowed to keep, and now this latest disaster!

Kermit looked as if he were going to throw up again. That's the way he reacts to things, whereas, although I'm three years older, I still tend to cry. But I didn't cry this time, even though I knew I would later on when I was alone. Instead, I stood up and stamped my foot again, but without the Spanish accent.

"If you go, then Ronald Reagan stays!" I shouted. And Ronald and I both ran out of the room.

# Chapter 2

I apologized to my father before I went
to bed because I didn't want him to get
the idea he meant no more to me than a
dog. Besides, the more I thought about a whole winter
with my father gone, the worse I felt.

"Are you sure we can't come with you?" I asked
him. "All the other times we went together. I bet you
misunderstood!"

"I'm afraid there's no mistake about it," my father
said. "The State Department thinks that some of the
places I'm going to visit aren't the safest places to bring a
wife and two children."

"How about just one child?" I asked. "I promise I
wouldn't get in your way. Besides, won't you need an
interpreter? I had six months of Spanish in fourth grade!"

My father just smiled and shook his head.

"What about riding?" I asked. "This means no more
riding!"

"No, it doesn't," said my father. "Your mother can
drive you out to the farm from time to time. You'll both

be welcome, and come to think of it, Kermit might like to learn too."

I wanted to scream. I wanted to shake my father and tell him that if I couldn't ride with him, just the two of us, I refused to ride at all, but I knew that wouldn't help, so I controlled myself.

"I'm going to miss you like crazy," I explained. "People who have been orphans need more affection than people who haven't. That's why I'll need Ronald more than ever if you're not here. She gives me affection."

"All Ronald Reagan has given you so far is a few extra fleas," my father said.

When my father tries to be funny, he isn't always very logical. "I got the fleas *because* of the affection," I pointed out. "It was what you call a package deal."

"Can't you get your affection from Kermit?" he asked.

"Kermit has fleas too," I told him. Apparently he didn't know about this yet because he looked a little upset. "Besides," I went on, "I don't want Kermit in my bed. Some people think he's cute, but I don't."

Then my father was really upset. "I absolutely forbid you to let that mutt sleep in your bed!" he shouted. "She sleeps downstairs and on the floor. I don't want black hairs all over the furniture."

I suggested getting black slipcovers. The ones we have now are Chinese white, and little things like licorice bubble gum tend to stick out like a sore thumb. Ronald's hair wouldn't show on black slipcovers, and we wouldn't have any more problems with the bubble gum either.

"Don't be silly," said my father. "The point is that we're not in a position to give a dog a good home."

I agreed it wasn't such a great home, but it would be a lot better once it had a dog in it. "I'll take care of Ronald," I said. "I'll do everything. I swear I will!"

But my father kept saying that Ronald had to go. He made me put the signs back on the trees, and I think he actually would have driven Ronald to the pound except that his mind was on his trip. So instead, my mother promised to put an ad in the local papers.

Meanwhile, school dragged on. I thought we had finished fractions by the end of fourth grade, but it turned out there were more, and they kept getting harder. When I mentioned it, the teacher said I would be doing fractions all my life. She didn't even look sorry.

I had to write my sevens tables on my fingers with ball point ink because you weren't allowed to look them up. My mother made me scrub everything off each day when I came back from school, but she didn't mind too much because she said if I wrote my sevens tables on my fingers every morning, I would end up knowing them. So far it hasn't worked.

Math wasn't the only problem in fifth grade. I was also having trouble with the other kids. After I got to be best friends with Parker, I hadn't bothered much about anybody else, so I stopped getting asked to birthday parties, and everybody kind of left me to myself.

"Why don't you ever bring a friend home from school?" my mother asked. "I hate to see you moping around, waiting for Parker every day."

I didn't mope. Waiting for Parker was the only

thing that made school bearable. I used to sit there during math thinking about whether her bus would be on time, whether I could sneak some food out to our clubhouse, and how I could persuade my mother to let us use the extra bathmat for a rug. Then I would go home and fight with Kermit a little if he was around, but he usually wasn't because he was friends with every kid within walking distance.

"Kermit is sociable," my mother told me. She didn't add that I wasn't, but I could see it in her face.

"I'm sociable too," I argued. "I'm sociable with Parker, and I'm sociable with Ronald Reagan. It's better to have two really deep friendships than to play fast and loose like Kermit."

"Nonsense!" said my mother. "Kermit is a normal, affectionate little boy."

Affectionate! Would you call affectionate someone who deliberately learns his sevens tables so that he can go around shouting them in your ear all day long? Not his tens or anything easy like that. Just his sevens. He even sings them to the music from *Star Wars* with this innocent expression on his face, and everyone thinks it's so cute.

"Eight *times*—seven is *fifty*-six!" And don't think I learned it from him that way. It happens to be written on my left pinky.

My mother had a point, though. If it was normal to have a million friends like Kermit, then I was just plain abnormal. I don't think I ever had more than one good friend at a time. The truth is, traveling around the world the way we did, I got to care more about having my own family around me. Even Kermit, bratty as he was. I just figured it must have been starting out as an orphan that made me so dependent on my family.

The problem was now that we were back in America with a place of our own, we didn't seem to be such a close family anymore. Kermit was usually at someone else's house, and now my father was going away for longer than he had ever been away from us before. I didn't know how I was going to stand it. Thank goodness I still had Parker!

Then all of a sudden I didn't even have Parker because she played a rotten trick on me.

She didn't call up after school one day, and when I went over to find out why, her mother said she had gone out with a friend. So I went to the clubhouse by myself, and when I got there, it had this sign on it.


PRIVATE CLUB!
MEMBERS ONLY!!!
VIOLATORS WILL BE TOWED


"Hey, that's a great sign!" I shouted. "Where did you get it?"

Parker shouted back, "Members only! Can't you read?"

"It's just me: Martha!" I said. I tried the door, but Parker had the hook on it, so it wouldn't open. Parker giggled, and so did someone else.

"Who have you got inside there?" I asked. "I thought this was private!"

"It is!" said Parker. "It's private, so you have to go to private school to belong. Get the point?"

It seemed kind of pointless to stand there shouting, so I went home.

From then on, every time I saw Parker she was with this other girl. I found out that her name was Jessica. She was new in the neighborhood, and she went to the same private school Parker did. I told Parker I didn't want anybody new in our clubhouse, but she just kept repeating that private clubs were for private schools.

"What's so great about private schools?" I asked my mother. "Parker acts as if public schools give you bad breath or something."

My mother said a lot of stuff about false values and about Parker's feeling perhaps a little conceited about being in an expensive school that's not too easy to get into. "When she gets her values straightened out, she'll look back and feel ashamed of herself," my mother said.

That sounded good, but meanwhile I was stuck with no friends at all. "I don't understand how you can be best friends with a person one day and the next day not even speak to her," I told my mother. "I just don't understand. What did I do wrong?"

"You didn't do anything wrong, sweetie," said my mother. "My guess is that Parker isn't as popular in her new school as she hoped to be, and she has the mistaken idea that she'll make new friends more easily by turning her back on the old ones. In any case, it's not your fault."

I knew she was just trying to make me feel better. The truth is that Parker is the kind of girl that's popular wherever she goes, and my mother knows it as well as I do.

I kept thinking there must be something I could do to make things all right again. Something short of switching to private school, that is. If only my father had been there, he might have helped. It was the kind of problem we could have discussed in the car, coming back from riding. Being a diplomat, my father was an expert with people. I wished I had inherited the gift, but I knew that was impossible because I was an orphan.

In any case I sat down and wrote a long letter telling my father all about it. "Answer quick!" I wrote. "Special delivery if you can. I need help fast!"

One good thing: Ronald Reagan was still with us, and I had gotten rid of the fleas. It was about. time because the second-grade teacher said that Kermit couldn't come to school anymore unless he brought a note from the doctor saying it wasn't chicken pox.

The more I got to know Ronald, the more I loved her, so the ad my mother was planning to put in the paper had me worried. All kinds of people read *The Georgetowner*, and one of them might be Ronald's owner. But there was nothing I could do about it except make Ronald sound like the kind of dog nobody would want.

I think my mother suspected something because when I asked her if I could write the ad, she said she'd rather do it herself, and she sealed the envelope. But she made one mistake: she gave me the letter to mail on my way to school. I put it in my bookbag. I put in a roll of Scotch tape too to seal it up when I got through with it.

*The Georgetowner* has a classified ad form that's all blocked out like a crossword puzzle. You get three lines for three dollars, and my mother had filled them in with ink, so I couldn't make any drastic changes.

I don't know why she put in that part about weekdays because we're always home on weekends too. Unless maybe she wanted to use up all the spaces she paid for. My mother is like that.

Anyway, I was hard put to think of a way to change that ad. I had been hoping to throw in an adjective like "repulsive," but there wasn't enough space, and if I ran over to the next line, it would cost another dollar. I wasn't about to make any changes on my mother's check. I mean, if they put me in prison for forgery, it would probably be one of those places where no dogs are allowed.

But after I stared at the ad for a while, it struck me that "yucky" has the same number of letters as "young," and I could just write over my mother's handwriting, which is what I did.

I jumbled the telephone number on purpose. Chances are some kid would be so crazy to have a black Lab that he wouldn't care whether Ronald was yucky or not. He would call up anyway and pretend she belonged to him. Knowing my mother, she wouldn't ask for proof, so I was playing it safe.

I was scared to death my mother would ask to see

the ad when the next issue of *The Georgetowner* came out, but as it happened, she had other things on her mind.

After my father had been gone for a month or so, my mother started getting bored. She is a psychiatric social worker, but she had been working only part time since we moved to Georgetown so that she would be free to do things with us at home. But nowadays all the cooking and housework were finished way before evening, and even after she coached me in math, my mother had a lot of time on her hands. Sometimes she would do things with her friends, but on the whole she was fidgety. Then one day she burst into the house looking as if she had just won a trip to Disneyworld.

"Guess what!" she said. "From now on I'm working full time!"

This was supposed to make me happy? All it meant was she wouldn't get home until six, and the cooking and housework and math would be crammed into the time between supper and bed.

"Who is going to vacuum?" I asked her.

I was pretty sure she hadn't thought about that, but it turned out she had. "*You* are," she said.

I assumed she was joking. Even Kermit thought it was a scream, and he started singing this stupid song to the music from *Star Wars*, naturally: "Mar-*tha*—vacuums the *bed*-room! Mar-*tha*—vacuums the *bath*-room!"

"Don't laugh," I advised him. "Do you know what this means? It means soup and crackers every night for dinner."

Kermit hates soup and crackers, which are what we always get when my mother comes home late. So that shut Kermit up pretty effectively, but my mother didn't like my reasoning.

"We all miss Daddy," she said, "and we're all finding different ways to cope with the way we feel. My way happens to be getting more involved in my work. Why can't we cooperate?"

"My way happens to be having a dog," I answered, "but who's cooperating with *me*?"

I shouldn't have opened my mouth. My mother stared at Ronald Reagan as if she hadn't seen her for a long time. "By the way," she said, "whatever became of that ad in *The Georgetowner*?"

"They printed it," I said. "It looks great! I'll run get it."

But I ran and got the vacuum cleaner instead and started doing the living room.

Our vacuum is about three hundred years old. It has been three times around the world, and it makes such a racket that the neighbors asked us not to use it after ten o'clock at night. I followed my mother around with it for a while until she decided to take Kermit down to Swensen's for a cone, just to get away from the noise.

I didn't mind. I liked ice cream, but the best ice cream in the world was at that place where I stopped with my father on the way home from riding. If I couldn't have that, I'd rather stay with Ronald. As for Ronald, she slunk upstairs and hid under my bed. She hates the vacuum.

It turned out not to be the meals or the vacuuming I minded so much as another change in my life: I had to go to an after-school group. Ten is certainly old enough to have your own key and be alone at home for a couple of hours, but my mother refused even to consider it.

"Knowing you, you'd take Ronald out for a walk and forget to lock the door," she said. "Besides, you know you hate to sit for Kermit."

"I'll wait until you get home to walk Ronald," I promised, "and I'll lock Kermit in his room."

"Gee, thanks!" said Kermit.

"Or wait, I have a better idea!" I said. "Kermit can go to an after-school group, and I'll come home with the key."

I could have gone on arguing for hours, but I noticed that my mother looked upset. I could tell she was beginning to wonder whether she'd be a better parent if she stayed home after all, and I started to feel sorry for her.

"Oh, never mind!" I said. "I think it's great you're working full time. As long as you're happy, that is. Personally, I'd hate it."

My mother signed us both up at Saint Michael's Church in Georgetown, and we had to start going the very next Monday. I didn't mind for myself so much as for Ronald. If you ask me, it was a little hard on her to keep her locked up indoors until six o'clock in the evening.

I mentioned the fact to my mother when she came up to say good night on Sunday. She just said it proved that we were the wrong kind of family for a dog.

"I know how much you care, Martha," she explained. "The problem is that the longer we keep Ronald, the harder it's going to be for you to give her up. That's why I want you to find a home for her before you grow too attached to her."

Attached! Ronald was the most important thing in my life, that was all.

"I bet my real parents would have let me have a dog!" I told my mother as she turned out the light.

Lying there in the dark, I imagined my reunion with my real parents. They'd be so glad to find me that they'd take me out of Saint Michael's and let me have a dog. Or maybe two dogs. I was still deciding what I'd choose for the second dog when I fell asleep.

# Chapter 3

One good thing about that after-school group: it made me like school a lot better by comparison. At school, unless it was physical ed, you didn't have to play kickball if you didn't feel like it. At school, if you finished your social studies before the other kids, you could read a book. But at dumb old Saint Michael's, we had to do everything all together, and believe me, all together included some of the world's greatest freaks.

Even if you needed to go to the girls' room, somebody else was supposed to go with you. Can you imagine raising your hand and asking, "Anybody else need to pee?" I was careful to stay away from the water fountain.

There were eighteen of us in the group. We had to line up in the playground at three o'clock and march over to Saint Michael's, where there is this big community room, kind of like a gym. There were two teachers to tell us what to do, named Larry and Sondra. They said not to call them teachers because they were just friends, but what kind of friends would boss you around for three hours a day, five days a week?

Larry carried a guitar wherever he went, even to the park, and Sondra was big on what she called creative expression. If there happened to be two seconds when we weren't doing something, Larry would call us over and start thumping his guitar, and Sondra would yell, "Come on, guys!" and hop around with her bottom stuck out. Then we were all supposed to sing and stick our bottoms out and reveal our true personalities.

I told Sondra that my true personality was sedentary, and she didn't even know what I meant.

"That means your bottom is for sitting on, not for wagging around the way Ronald wags her tail," I told her. She didn't even bother to ask who Ronald was.

On sunny days we went to Volta Park, and we had to walk over there in twos. Everyone had a "buddy" the whole time we were in the park. When Larry blew his whistle, you were supposed to find your buddy and hold his or her hand up in the air to show you weren't lost.

My buddy was usually one of the Rodriguez twins. Their names were Aurora and Amelia, but I called them both "Aurelia." They were twin jerks. The thing they thought was the most fun in the whole world was getting people mixed up about who they were. When I was supposed to have Amelia for my buddy, I would get Aurora, and when I was supposed to get Aurora, I would end up with Amelia. They thought this was hysterical.

"Look here, Aurelias," I used to say. "You look alike, you talk alike, you even smell alike, so who cares which is which? It isn't funny—it's just boring."

But the Rodriguez twins never thought anything was boring. They even got a kick out of playing bingo. Bingo is what we did on rainy days, and it was compulsory. If you won, you got a prize, and the prize for girls was always play makeup. I asked if I could read a book instead, but Sondra said, "We like to do things together."

"Why can't we ever read books together?" I asked.

"We will someday," she promised. But the other kids said they'd rather play bingo.

When I mentioned this to my mother, she said I wasn't being cooperative. "Think of Saint Michael's as a miniature democracy," she said. "You may not like the majority decision, but you tolerate it because you agreed to stick together."

I told her that sounded like something out of my social studies book, but it didn't sound like what you hear on the news. "I was forced into this, remember?" I said. "Besides, what about minority rights?"

Right away my mother got that worried look in her eyes again—the one I'm such a sucker for because I always back down when she gets it.

"Martha, sweetie," she said, "is it really so terrible? Would it really make you and Kermit happier if I came home in the afternoon?"

I backed down. Sure it would make me happier, but I didn't want anyone accusing me of making my mother quit her job, especially now that she was beginning to act a little happier herself.

"It's not so much Saint Michael's," I told her. "It's just me. I happen to have a thing about privacy."

My mother lost the worried look and laughed. "I wish I knew what turned you out such a loner! Your father and Kermit and I all seem to thrive on company. I can't imagine whom you got it from!"

From my real parents, that's who. What could be more obvious? I didn't argue the point, though. I just suffered through Saint Michael's by keeping my mind on six P.M. when we got out and I could take Ronald up to the park for a run.

Ronald had a leash that I was supposed to use when we went out, but the clip didn't work too well, so it was a pain to get on and off. Instead, I used this old rope that was about twice as long as the leash. Ronald liked it better.

Well, one day toward the end of October I was on my way to the park when who should come down the sidewalk but Bettysue Parker Ames. In person. She was looking down at her feet, so she didn't see me until Ronald bounced up and licked her face. I tried to teach Ronald not to do this, especially to Parker, but Ronald has a heart like a marshmallow.

"Hi!" I said. "What happened? Did you lose your shadow?" Meaning Jessica.

As usual, Parker didn't hear me. She just pointed at the rope. "What's that thing for?"

"It's a leash," I said. "L-E-A-S-H. Didn't you ever see one before?"

"It looks more like a dirty old R-O-P-E to me," she said. Very funny.

"Come on, Ronald," I said. "Let's go." But Ronald kept on licking Parker's face. Parker probably just got through eating a Hershey bar. Ronald loves chocolate.

"Why do you keep her tied up like that?" Parker asked.

How stupid can you get? "This happens to be a busy street," I said. "There happen to be a lot of cars going by. You know, *cars*? I don't happen to want Ronald to get run over."

"She wouldn't get run over. She's too smart," said Parker.

She was probably right, but the trouble was that after being cooped up inside all day, Ronald Reagan got a little wild. She would race forward a mile a minute, put on her brakes, and come scooting back. She bounced around like a black kangaroo, and I just didn't trust her until she got to the park and worked off some of that energy.

"It's cruelty to animals to tie them up with a rope," said Parker. "Somebody should report you. It's against the law."

I wondered if she were right. I also wondered why she didn't mind her own business. "I can't let her go. It isn't safe," I said.

Parker laughed this big fake laugh. "You're just afraid she'll run home to her real owner," she said.

"She doesn't have a real owner. I mean, *I'm* her real owner," I told her. "If somebody took her a hundred miles away, she'd still find her way back to me." I read a book about a dog that did that, and Ronald is a million times smarter than that dog.

Parker just said, "You're chicken."

We were getting close to the park, so I untied Ronald's rope, but I didn't want Parker to think she had bullied me into it, so I walked ahead, sort of humming. And what does Ronald do? She goes crazy. She skids back and forth a couple of times, then turns about seven somersaults, and shoots across to the park just when this pick-up truck comes tearing down the street.

The truck slammed on its brakes, but there was a green station wagon behind, which crashed into the truck. Nothing serious, but there were some broken headlights, and a man got out of the station wagon and started yelling at the man in the truck.

Right away I recognized the man in the station wagon. He was a neighbor. I looked around for Parker, but she had disappeared, so I disappeared too. After I caught up with Ronald, I took the long way home.

You would think this was enough trouble for one day, but that wasn't all. I got home and had supper, and then I had to vacuum Kermit's room. That vacuuming business turned out to be no joke, but I must admit the house was cleaner than before my mother started working full time. One thing is sure: when I grow up, I'm going to have kids right away so they can work for me and leave me free for my career.

I always leave Kermit's room for last because it's the worst. First I have to move his train tracks, and I'm lucky if I don't get electrocuted. Then I have to shake out his sheets and all those locomotives he takes to bed with him to get the Cheetos out. I used to think math was hard, but fractions are nothing compared to shaking the Cheetos out of eight locomotives.

Well, I was just finishing Kermit's room when the phone rang. Nobody answered because my mother and Kermit were out buying a cone at Swensen's. Every time I vacuum they go to Swensen's for a cone. It's a wonder Kermit is so skinny!

I finally got to the phone myself, and this man's

voice asked whether we had a black Lab. It wasn't a particularly pleasant voice. I said yes, we did have a black Lab, but she was yucky and repulsive, so it probably wasn't the same black Lab he was looking for. All the time I was talking, I wondered how he'd found the right number.

The guy didn't give up. He just said, "May I please speak to your mother?"

"Could you call back?" I asked. "She's in the bathroom."

So he hung up. Meanwhile, I turned the television on loud and pinched my nose and tried to make my voice sound like a grownup's. "Speaking!" I said when I answered the phone for the second time.

He hadn't asked to speak to anyone yet, but I wanted to make it sound convincing. There was a pause. Then he asked, "Is this Mrs. Albright? You people have a black Labrador retriever, don't you?"

"Why yes, we do!" I said, trying to get that middle-aged lilt into my voice. "How extraordinary you should ask! But I'm afraid Ronald Reagan can't come to the phone. She's at the vet's for contagious mange."

There was a longer pause. Then the man said, "Thank you, I'll call back when your mother is at home." And he did.

My mother wasn't happy. Personally I think she stays in a bad mood for about three hours after every cone because she wishes she hadn't eaten one. It isn't as if she were built like Kermit. I keep telling her she'll end up like the fat lady in the circus, but she has no self-control. I even suggested buying a new vacuum so we could all stay home together, but she said she'd rather spend the money on ice cream. What can you do with a mother like that?

Anyway, when my mother finished talking with the man, I could see I was in trouble. It wasn't someone answering the ad after all; it was the man in the station wagon.

"Do you realize you were responsible for what might have been a fatal accident this afternoon?" my mother asked.

"It was only fatal to two headlights," I said.

"Why was Ronald off her leash?" she wanted to know.

"Why was that man driving so fast?" I asked back.

My mother said that my father would have a fit if he knew we hadn't gotten rid of that crazy dog yet, and I said anyone would act crazy after being cooped up indoors until six.

"I know how Ronald feels," I told her. "I feel just the same after I get out of Saint Michael's."

"Don't tell me you're still complaining about Saint Michael's!" said my mother. "Why, Kermit enjoys it!"

"Kermit isn't an orphan," I said.

Well, the days went by, and they were all pretty much the same: school and Saint Michael's and vacuuming when I got home, and the whole time I had this little ache inside because I knew Ronald would have to go. My mother tried to cheer me up by offering to drive me out to the farm, but I refused. I told her that riding was no fun without my father. Besides, I was crazy about dogs, not horses. Then one day something new happened. It was about a week before Halloween.

It was one of those days when not one single thing

went right, starting with the alarm not going off. My mother woke me at eight-forty, which left ten minutes to eat breakfast and remember where I left my science homework.

Kermit had come down at eight, as usual. He finished the Sugar Corn Pops, so I had to have raisin bran. We made it to school on time, but it turned out that what I thought was my science homework was the letter I was writing to the president about eliminating math in public schools. The science teacher gave me a zero.

Then when I needed to go to the girls' room before lunch, Gloria Vasquez came too, and she said we should see what the boys' room was like. There were all these little sinks, and we were just washing our hands when Carlos Sanchez came in. He's only in first grade, and he started screaming.

The principal wouldn't believe me when I said I was running a sociological survey, and she made us stay in during recess. That made me late for Spanish, so the Spanish teacher gave out all the best parts in the Christmas play and I had to be a mushroom. I didn't even know the Spanish word for mushroom.

After that we had physical ed, and it was kickball. It's bad enough jumping up and down and clapping your hands over your head, but at least everyone else is doing it too. In kickball each person does something different, and I never can remember what I'm supposed to do. Someone is always yelling, "Stay on base!" or "Get out of the way, stupid!"

This time just when I was wondering whether I had filled Ronald's water bowl, someone yelled, "Kick it, Martha!"

I kicked, and the ball went up in the air and landed in the basketball net, where it stuck, naturally, while the other team got three runs. Mr. Butt, the physical ed teacher, was really nice about it. He said it was a kind of miracle, and if I tried to do it on purpose, I couldn't in a million years. But our team lost the game.

When the bell rang at three o'clock, all I could think about was putting my arms around Ronald. When things go wrong, I always tell her about it, because she wags her tail as if she were saying, "I don't know what you're talking about, but it can't be very important."

But I had to go to my dumb after-school group, so there were three more hours to live through before I could hug Ronald. Then it struck me that I really didn't have to go to Saint Michael's. Lots of the kids would skip a day if they had a dentist appointment or something, and I was pretty sure I could bribe Kermit to keep a secret.

Kermit was standing in line, playing this stupid game with the Rodriguez twins where he shut his eyes and they would switch around and he would guess which one was which. I pulled him out of line and held my fist about an inch in front of his nose.

"See this?" I asked him. "If you tell Larry and Sondra that I played hooky from Saint Michael's this afternoon, you're going to get this right in the kisser. But if you don't tell, I'll buy you a Hershey bar."

"It's a deal," said Kermit. For a seven-year-old he catches on fast.

Larry wasn't too pleased when I said I had to go to the dentist. I told him my mother promised she would call up Saint Michael's about it, and she must have forgotten. I tried to look really upset, so Larry let me go.

I didn't have a key to our house, but you can get in if you climb over the back fence and jiggle the kitchen window until the catch slips. It's easy; even Kermit can do it.

The whole time I was jiggling, I could see Ronald jumping around on the other side of the window. She got so excited that she began to leak all over the kitchen floor. I could tell she wasn't going to be able to wait until six o'clock for her walk, so I got the rope, and we went out again.

Just as I was about to shut the front door, I had this sudden urge to wear my gold chain. I'm not supposed to wear it unless I'm going someplace where my mother is going too because she's afraid I'll lose it.

I don't like charm bracelets and silly jewelry like that, but this chain was pretty nice even if it did say "Martha," so I went upstairs and put it on. After that Ronald and I ran as fast as our legs would carry us until all the bad part of the day drained out of us and we were both exhausted.

We stopped, and Ronald flopped down on the sidewalk, panting. I checked to make sure my chain was still there, and when I touched it, I remembered how really mad my mother was going to be.

I must have looked worried because suddenly this deep voice near me said, "Grin!"

For a minute I thought it was Ronald talking, and I jumped about three feet in the air. Then I noticed an old man sitting on a brick wall, with an old lady right next to him. The wall was in front of a little wooden house painted yellow with white shutters, and there were a lot of flowers and things planted all around. It was really pretty.

"Did you say something?" I asked.

The old man glared at me and repeated:

> "If you're up against a bruiser and you're getting knocked about—
>> Grin.
> If you're feeling pretty groggy, and you're licked beyond a doubt—
>> Grin."

"Oh!" I said. "Okay."

He seemed a little weird, so I started to move along, but the old lady said, "That's a very pretty necklace, dear."

"Oh, thanks!" I said. I could tell she wanted to get a closer look at it, so I went back.

She started fingering my chain, and she said, "Lovely, dear. And the finest gold!"

I was sure she was going to ask why my mother let me wear it when I was walking the dog, but it seemed she was one grownup in a million who minded her own business.

"Thanks," I said. "I guess my mother must have paid a lot for it."

The old man gave a kind of snort and said, " 'A fool and his money are soon parted.' "

"I beg your pardon?" I said. I thought he must be a bit cuckoo.

" 'A fool and his money are soon parted,' " he repeated. "Calvin Coolidge. Best president this country ever had."

"Oh," I said. "Did Calvin Coolidge say to grin, too?"

"No," said the old man with this smug look on his face. "That was Robert Service. Finest poet this country ever had."

"Can you say the rest of it?" I asked.

The old man looked smugger than ever. "I'll give you 'The Cremation of Sam McGee'," he said. "Since you're interested in good poetry."

At first I thought he was going to give me a book, but instead he stood up, got this faraway look in his eyes, and began to recite in a singsong voice. The old lady got a faraway look in her eyes too, but more as if she were thinking about her grocery list.

I didn't see how she could be bored. 'The Cremation of Sam McGee' was the most exciting poem I ever heard in my life. I bet if they showed it on TV, you would need parental guidance to watch it. I mean, it was downright gory!

"Thank you!" I said. "That was fantastic!"

The old man bobbed his head up and down. "Beats all your namby-pamby verse-makers to a pulp," he said. "Shakespeare could never have written that, could he, Maud?"

The old lady smiled and said, "No, dear," but I could tell her mind was on something else, and I was right because she touched my chain again and said, "Martha. What a pretty name! Are you Martha?"

Pretty? It takes all tastes to make a world! "Martha Albright," I said, "and this is Ronald Reagan."

That was when the old man introduced himself. He said his name was Amory Able, and Maud was his wife.

"Do you live here?" I asked, pointing at the little wooden house.

Amory Able nodded. "That's right. We've lived in that house for fifty years, and you couldn't find a nicer place in the whole of Georgetown."

"But it's lonely now that Arabella is gone," said Maud with a sad look on her face.

"That's too bad," I said. "Who was Arabella?"

"Our daughter," said Amory Able. "She left us in 1970."

He looked sad too. I felt really sorry for them. It was obvious they had been crazy about this Arabella and just couldn't get over her running away from home, even though it was more than ten years ago. "That's terrible!" I said. "Do you have any other children?"

Amory Able shook his head.

"Arabella is a nice name," I said. "I wish my parents had called me Arabella."

Maud smiled a little. "My daughter thought Arabella was too fancified. She used to say if she had a daughter of her own, she would call her something plain, like Martha. They say the grass is always greener on the other side of the fence!"

Amory Able glared at her. "Poppycock!" he snapped. "Who says that? It can't have been Calvin Coolidge!"

"I was just using a figure of speech, dear," said Maud.

"Then don't!" said Amory Able.

I wasn't about to stand there listening to them argue. Besides, it was getting late. "I have to go now!" I said. "I'm supposed to be at my after-school group, so I have to get back before my mother finds out I'm not."

I wondered why I told them that when they didn't even ask, but I found out later they were the kind of people you tell things to. Anyway, they didn't look shocked.

But when Ronald and I were about half a block away, I heard Amory Able shouting:

> "O, *what a tangled web we weave,*
> *When first we practice to deceive!*

"Calvin Coolidge!"

I was tempted to go back and argue the point, but just then I had the most fantastic idea, so I started running toward home so fast that Ronald could hardly keep up with me. I needed to think things over!

# Chapter 4

On the whole it had been a lucky day. Think of all the terrible things that could have happened! I might have lost my chain, for one, but I didn't. Somebody might have robbed our house because when I went out with Ronald, I left the door unlocked, but nobody did. Kermit could have told on me at Saint Michael's, but he had other things on his mind. My mother never even asked about my day at school because there was a letter from my father in the mail, and she couldn't talk about anything else all evening.

To go back a little, I got home about five o'clock after meeting the Ables. I locked the front door, put my chain back in my mother's jewel box, and gave Ronald some fresh water in her bowl. Then I climbed out the kitchen window and ran back to Saint Michael's Church to wait for Kermit. My timing was perfect. When my mother drove by to pick us up, she thought I had been playing bingo and prancing around with my bottom stuck out all afternoon.

I was afraid Kermit would let something slip, but he was too excited to remember I hadn't been at Saint Michael's. That was the day he won the giant jackpot at bingo.

"What did you get?" I asked him.

He showed me. It was this pink plastic vanity case with a mirror and a comb and brush and a lot of play makeup and a bottle of perfume inside. Perfume! "That's a girl's prize," I told him.

"They let me choose," said Kermit. "This looked like more fun than the doctor's kit."

He sure had a lot of fun with it too. First, he used up the makeup by drawing pink and blue stripes all over his body. They didn't wear off for a whole week, not even when I used Ajax on him, and the second-grade teacher sent my mother a note about it.

Kermit traded the comb and brush to a girl in his class for the cork out of her Thermos, which was smart thinking because he had lost his and he would have been in real trouble with my mother when she found out. He poked a lot of holes in the vanity case and kept his tent caterpillars inside, and he spilled the perfume in his bed. That was the best part because the bed stank so much, even after my mother washed the sheets, that Ronald wouldn't sleep in Kermit's bed for days.

Anyway, what with Kermit's winning the jackpot and my mother's getting her letter from South America, nothing was said about my adventures that day. But privately I was thinking so hard that it gave me a headache.

What happened to Arabella? Did she ever have a little girl that she named something plain? Maybe she named her Martha. You can't get any plainer than Martha. Why, maybe she even had green eyes! And in that case, Maud and Amory Able were my grandparents.

The more I thought about it, the more convinced I was. This Arabella probably ran away from home and got married. Much as I enjoyed talking with Amory Able, I could see that he would be a difficult person to live with.

Maybe Arabella was hanging around the Potomac River one day and fell in love with a green-eyed sailor who liked privacy, and they lifted anchor and sailed away, just like that. It was the kind of thing I would do myself, only there aren't many sailors walking around Georgetown, and I'm not allowed to go down to the Potomac alone to look for one.

But suppose that's what happened to Arabella, and she got married and had a baby called Martha, and it was me?

The rest was harder to figure out, but not impossible. The most likely was that we were all out sailing when I was a tiny baby, and the boat capsized in a storm. My parents tied me on this big life buoy and set me adrift, and the buoy washed up on a beach. Someone found it with this tiny green-eyed baby in it, which was me, and no way of knowing who she was.

There were a number of things to check on before I could prove my theory. I decided to start by getting my mother to discuss the subject seriously.

"Something really interesting happened today," I told her. "I think I've got a clue to who I really am."

She didn't even take her eyes off my father's letter.

"Listen to this," she said. "Daddy says he already speaks Spanish like a native!"

"Why can't you tell me the truth?" I asked her. "Ten is old enough to know."

My mother sighed and looked up. "Sweetie, don't you think ten is old enough to stop believing in fairy tales too? I mean, everybody loves to fantasize, but enough is enough!"

"This isn't a fairy tale. This is real life!" I told her. "Listen, I think maybe I've found my true grandparents!"

My mother laughed. "Your true grandparents are alive and well in Portland, Oregon."

I glared at her.

> "O, *what a tangled web we weave,*
> *When first we practice to deceive!*

"Calvin Coolidge," I said.

"No," my mother said firmly. "That's Sir Walter Scott."

I didn't believe her, but I checked it out in our dictionary of quotations, and she was right. What's more, Calvin Coolidge didn't say that a fool and his money are soon parted, either. Someone called James Howell did. It confirmed my suspicion that Amory Able was a little cuckoo. Cuckoo, but nice. I decided to go back as soon as I could and ask him a few questions about Arabella, just sort of casually, without getting his hopes up before I was sure. But anxious as I was to unravel the mystery of my birth, there was more urgent business on hand. That was Halloween.

I know some people think trick-or-treating is only for really little kids, but I always get a kick out of dressing up, and our neighborhood is fantastic for loot. There are all these rich people who are so scared of finding shaving cream on their brass knockers that they have their butlers stand out with silver trays, and you can take as much as you want.

I didn't move to Georgetown until January, but Parker told me all about it, back when we were best friends. We even decided what we were going to be, and we had already planned our costumes. Parker was going to be a plumber, and I was going to be the plumber's friend.

Kermit said he had a better idea. "Let's be the musicians of Bremen," he said. "You can be the donkey, and I'll be the cat, and Ronald can be the dog, and we can climb on each other's backs and sing."

It wasn't such a bad idea. "Who is going to be the rooster?" I asked.

Kermit said we could make a rooster out of paper and tie it to Ronald's back, but it sounded too complicated. The act would take a lot of practice, and by the time we climbed on each other's backs, people would get tired of waiting. Even if they didn't, we'd be in a bad position to grab their candy. I decided to go back to my original idea of the plumber's friend. Besides, I already had what I needed for the costume.

Luckily the thirty-first was a warm night, and it wasn't raining because nothing looks stupider than Wonder Woman in rubbers or a skeleton with an umbrella. We must have looked dumb enough as it was. I mean, my costume was terrific, but my mother made me take

Kermit with me. All Kermit ended up doing was wrapping himself in about a dozen sheets.

"What are you supposed to be?" I asked. "A fat ghost?"

"No," said Kermit, "I'm mashed potatoes."

"That's stupid," I said. "Who's going to guess? And why would a plumber's friend be walking around with mashed potatoes? You'll spoil my act."

But my mother made me take him anyway, and she gave him this wooden spoon to hold, as if that made it any better. Everywhere we went people asked Kermit what he was supposed to be, and when he said mashed potatoes, they laughed their heads off and gave him an extra handful of candy. It was annoying, to say the least.

To make it worse, I kept having to run after Ronald because she was really upset when she saw all these kids dressed up like Wonder Woman, and she got a little fierce with some of them.

Ronald didn't actually bite anyone, at least only their clothes. But the parents weren't too pleased about it, and a lot of the kids started crying. So there I was hopping around in my handle, which was just a lot of brown wrapping paper wound around my legs. I could hardly see out of the plunger part, and Ronald kept tripping me up with her rope every time she took a lunge at Wonder Woman. Meanwhile, Kermit got all the loot.

Well, we had worked ourselves about four blocks up 34th Street when who should come around the corner but the plumber. I could have died! I mean, whoever would have guessed Parker would go on and be a plumber all the same after what had happened between us? What was she trying to prove?

43

I thought it showed really bad taste, and her costume wasn't even that great. She had on these old clothes her father wears around the house to do repairs, and she was carrying a toolbox to put her loot in. So does that make her a plumber? Her costume was completely pointless unless I went around with her, and that was out of the question.

"I hope you don't plan to follow *me* around!" I told her.

"I wouldn't trick-or-treat with you if you paid me a million dollars!" Parker said. "Your costume stinks."

"At least people can tell what I am," I said. "You just look like your father, and nobody knows who he is anyway."

As a matter of fact, Parker's father is a reporter, and you see him all the time on TV, so I wasn't being very truthful, but I was so mad I didn't care.

I guess Parker got mad too because she changed her mind and said, "This is a free country. You can't stop me from going where I want!"

Whenever we knocked on a door, Parker turned up too. I tried to pretend I didn't know her, but Ronald made a fool of herself as usual by licking Parker's face every time she got anywhere near us. Parker gave Ronald some chocolate, which didn't help. It was the first time I ever wished I had left Ronald at home.

"Where's Jessica?" I asked. "I bet she's all dolled up like Miss America!" But Parker pretended she didn't hear me.

Well, we kept on going from door to door like that, and the next thing I knew, we were standing in front of the little yellow house with white shutters. There wasn't any pumpkin out or anything, and there was only one window lit, upstairs. We usually skip places like that, but Parker rang the bell. I felt kind of sorry for the Ables.

"There's nobody home," I said. "Let's go to that place across the street."

The place across the street was one of these big brick mansions with two stone lions outside the front door. There was a maid in a black dress and a frilly white apron handing out the loot. Maybe next Halloween I'll be a maid or a butler.

But Parker kept on ringing the Ables' doorbell. I yanked on Ronald's rope, but just then Maud Able, holding a basket, opened the door and offered us each an apple. An apple! Kermit said thank you, but Parker was a little upset, and I could hardly blame her. I mean, it's better to turn off your lights than to give out apples. The only thing worse is these people who pour you a glass of cider and expect you to drink it on the spot.

Parker took an apple and put it in her toolbox, but she pulled this big can of shaving cream out of her pocket and squirted it all over the rest of the apples in Maud's basket. Then she ran.

I felt like running too, but Ronald wound her rope around my legs again because she had just caught sight of three more kids in Wonder Woman costumes. So I was stuck there, and Maud Able smiled at me and said, "Hello, Martha!" before she went back inside and shut the door.

It ruined my evening. I told Kermit I was going home, and his bag was full anyway, so he said okay.

When I lay in bed that night, eating candy corn and

listening to the big kids that rattle your knocker and yell after all your lights are out, I kept thinking about Maud Able's face when she saw the shaving cream on her apples. Even though I had nothing to do with it, I felt I owed her an apology. Halloween was on a Saturday that year, so there was one day left before I had to go to school. I promised myself I wouldn't let that day go by without paying a visit to Maud.

We don't go to church very regularly in my family, but I was afraid the Ables did. Besides, my mother says it's impolite to bother people on a Sunday morning. I waited until after lunch, and then I took Ronald out for a walk. Luckily Kermit was at a friend's house. I wasn't about to let Kermit in on my private affairs.

The Ables weren't sitting on their brick wall this time, so I rang their bell. Amory Able opened the door. He was holding an onion and an open penknife. I had been wondering what to say, but as it turned out, I didn't have to say anything. The minute Ronald saw Amory Able, she put her paws on his chest and started licking his face like crazy. I didn't know she was that fond of him. He hadn't paid any attention to her the first time they met.

Amory Able pushed Ronald away. "Down, boy, down!" he snapped.

I pulled on Ronald's rope. "She's a girl," I said.

"So I see," said Amory Able. "That's no excuse for bad manners. No dog of mine ever had bad manners."

"How many dogs have you had?" I asked.

"More than I can count," said Amory Able. "Wish I had one now. Dog is a man's best friend."

I couldn't have agreed with him more. I felt more

courageous knowing that we both liked dogs, so I asked if his wife was at home.

"She went shopping for some gewgaw or other," he told me. " 'A fool and his money are soon parted.' Calvin Coolidge."

I thought it safer not to contradict him. "Will she be back soon?" I asked.

"Ought to be," said Amory Able. "There aren't that many shops open on a Sunday. Have you had lunch?"

"Not to speak of," I said. I wasn't really hungry, but I wanted to keep my options open.

"I'm cooking mine," he said. "Might learn a thing or two by watching me while you wait. 'All things come to him who hustles while he waits.' Calvin Coolidge."

I watched him and he was right. I learned enough to keep me out of a kitchen for the next twenty years. He was slamming the pots and pans around and taking these weird things out of the refrigerator, and all the time he kept talking, talking, talking. He must have needed company really badly.

"Some people wouldn't go to this trouble," he told me. "Some people would go out and buy a cheeseburger. Horrible concoctions, cheeseburgers. Sure way to curdle your guts. It beats me why people go on eating that kind of trap. Why, some places people will pay as much as five dollars for a cheeseburger. Five dollars! What I'm making now doesn't cost a cent, practically speaking. It's all leftovers. Maud wanted to throw them out."

I asked what it was. If he was planning to use everything he put out on the counter, it would be garbage soup.

"Potato recipe," said Amory Able, "but it varies according to your ingredients."

He snapped his penknife shut and pulled out the screwdriver attachment. "Pot handle loose again," he said. "That's Maud. You'll find that some people won't spend a matter of thirty seconds learning something that may serve them all their lives. I hope you're not one of these women who let the handles loosen up on pots and pans just because they're too bone lazy to tighten the screws once in a while."

I told him I wasn't. I sat as far away as I could from him because I didn't want to get in his way. He shut the screwdriver attachment and opened the blade again.

"Always use my penknife when I'm cooking," he told me. "Women don't know how to keep a sharp edge on a kitchen knife."

He started cutting up the things on the counter: onions and potatoes with their skins still on, two over-ripe bananas and some salami, and these unappetizing things that looked like white carrots with congealed grease all over them.

Amory Able turned the gas up high. "First you want to get your pan hot, but not too hot," he said. "I hope you're not one of these women who burn the bottoms out of their saucepans before they even get started."

I told him I wasn't. I was fascinated. What kind of recipe calls for salami and bananas?

"Do you want me to peel those onions for you?" I asked.

Amory Able glared at me and said the skin was the best part. Then he threw in the white things, which I found out were leftover boiled turnips.

"I don't hold with herbs," he informed me. "They tend to foul up the taste. But if you throw in your leftover lima beans or something in that line, it gives a nice flavor."

It sounded like a useful recipe. We always have left over lima beans in our house because Kermit and I can't stand them. The question was: Would we like them any better this way?

"Is it soup?" I asked.

"Stew," said Amory Able.

He threw in the bananas. Then he opened the broom closet and reached for a slotted spoon that was hanging next to a fly swatter. "Learn to keep things where they belong, and you'll know where to find them," he snapped at me.

I promised I would. He threw in the salami and stirred. I had to admit it smelled pretty good. Then he started chopping up some Swiss cheese, rind and all. I didn't think you were supposed to eat the rind, but when I mentioned it, Amory Able said the rind was the best part. Then he got out a little bottle and sloshed in this red stuff that looked like grape juice.

"Port wine," he said when I asked him. "I don't hold with alcohol, but a little port wine livens up your potato recipe."

He gave one more stir, slammed the lid on the pot, turned the gas down low, and sat next to me on a kitchen stool. "Now, tell me what's on your conscience," he said.

I didn't know what to say. I wasn't sure whether Maud had told him about the shaving cream. If she hadn't, I didn't see why I should.

"Better get it off your chest," said Amory Able. "What is it, school?"

I said that school was pretty bad, but nothing out of the ordinary, and there wasn't much I could do about it except grow up fast.

"That's the attitude!" he said, bobbing his head up and down. "Education is a necessary evil, but it won't teach you the important things in life. Robert Service put it well:

> "*I would rather be a fool*
>    *Living in my Paradise,*
>    *Than the leader of a school,*
> *Sadly sane and weary wise.*"

I thought that was pretty good, and I asked him if he would write it down for me. It might come in handy the next time I had a run-in with the principal.

"Learn it by heart," he advised me. "Poetry can come in handy, especially if you're planning to make a speech."

I said I wasn't planning any speeches, but he went and got me this book all the same and showed me the page. While I was looking at it, he took out two bowls and served the stew. It still smelled okay, but it didn't look too good. I began to wish I hadn't said I'd wait for Maud.

"I just ate seven peanut-butter-and-jelly sandwiches," I told him.

"Mistake," he said. "Sure way to curdle your guts. You'll feel better when you've had a little of this."

So I had to taste it, and believe me, it tasted pretty awful. It was all I could do to keep from spitting. When Amory Able wasn't looking, I offered it to Ronald Reagan, but Ronald wouldn't even try. At first I thought maybe Amory Able had made a mistake in the recipe, but he seemed to think it was just fine because he had seconds and thirds. When he got through, he stared at the pot with this sad look on his face, as if he were dying for some more if only he had room.

While Amory Able was eating, I leafed through the Robert Service book to see if I could find something interesting. It was a really good book. I read this gruesome poem called "Lipstick Liz" about how a lady does in her man along with another lady the man likes better than Lipstick Liz. Then I read another, even better, called "Barb-Wire Bill." Just as I got through that, Maud Able walked in.

I felt really sorry for Maud because the kitchen was such a mess, and all there was for her lunch was banana-salami stew, but she didn't seem to mind. She just cleared a place on the counter for her packages and sat down with a happy sigh.

"Such beautiful weather!" she said. "I could have stayed out all day."

"Lucky I didn't give you more money, then," said Amory Able. "Want some stew?"

Maud lifted the lid and sniffed at the stew. "No thank you, dear," she said. "I'll make myself a cup of tea." Then she smiled at me. "It was nice of you to pay us a visit, Martha dear."

Did she really mean it, or was she trying to make

me feel guilty? I decided to get the apology over with right away. "I'm really sorry about that shaving cream, Mrs. Able," I said. "I didn't know my friend had it with her. As a matter of fact, she isn't my friend anymore. But even if she were, I wouldn't have wanted her to do it to you."

I thought I was embarrassed, but you should have seen Maud's face. She was positively blushing. You would have thought she played the trick herself! "Think no more about it, dear," she said. "I'm sure you weren't responsible for the circumstances."

Amory Able was having none of that. " 'Men are always blaming their circumstances for what they are. There are no circumstances,' " he told me. "Do you have any idea who said that?"

"Calvin Coolidge?" I guessed, and I got up to leave. "I'm sorry," I said, "but I have to go home now. Thanks for the stew. And thanks a *lot* for letting me read your book!"

Then I remembered the second thing I had come about. I couldn't think of any subtle way to introduce the subject, so I came straight out and asked, "By the way, did Arabella run away with a green-eyed sailor?"

Amory Able snorted, but Maud didn't seem to find it strange at all. From the way she smiled, I thought for a minute I must have hit on the truth, but I was out of luck again. "No dear," said Maud. "She didn't."

Amory Able showed me to the door. "I'm glad you enjoyed the stew," he said. "It's an easy recipe. Come in useful someday when you have a family of your own. All you do is take an onion or two and a couple of ripe

bananas, and if you happen to have some leftover ruta-
baga—"

He stood in his doorway talking until I got to the
end of the block and turned the corner. Even then I
could hear him for a while. It made me feel a little dizzy,
but that might have been the stew.

# Chapter
# 5

I was a little discouraged when my sailor theory collapsed, but I was still convinced that the Ables must be my grandparents. I just knew they were.

For one thing, Amory Able and I were both crazy about dogs. No one in my adoptive family cared that much about dogs, not even Kermit, and I must have inherited it from *someone*. It occurred to me that maybe Arabella ran away with a dog trainer. I would have to go back and ask Maud.

It was harder than I expected to go off by myself and visit the Ables. I knew it was no use trying to pull another dentist appointment on Larry and Sondra. If I skipped Saint Michael's again, I would need a note from my mother. And most evenings when I went out to walk Ronald, my mother made me take Kermit with me. It was getting dark early, and she said it wasn't safe to walk alone.

"I'm not alone when I'm with Ronald," I argued. "If someone tried to attack me, she'd bite."

"If Ronald met the devil himself, she'd lick his face," my mother told me, and I had to admit she was right. Ronald is no watchdog; she's too friendly.

"Well, what good would Kermit do?" I asked her. "He's smaller than I am, and he's scared of the dark."

"Kermit can make a lot of noise," my mother reminded me. "It's safer to take him along, given the circumstances."

" 'Men are always blaming their circumstances for what they are. There are no circumstances,' " I told her. "Calvin Coolidge."

"No. George Bernard Shaw," she said.

I didn't contradict her. I didn't even bother to look it up. She was probably right again. In any case, she got her way. When I went out, Kermit went too, and every time anyone came near us, Kermit would scream. We never met anyone except neighbors walking other dogs, and they didn't appreciate the screaming. It was kind of embarrassing.

That left only weekends for getting off by myself, but on weekends I had another problem. Wherever I went, by some freak of chance Parker would turn up. If I went to the drugstore, a few minutes later she'd be there too. If I took Ronald for a run in Volta Park, we'd hardly have time to go once around the field before she came out of the bushes kicking a soccer ball. All I had to do was walk down the block, and by coincidence, Parker would come out her front door. I began to think I was jinxed.

"Are you trailing me or something?" I asked her one day when she just happened to be at Swensen's too buying a cone.

"This is a free country, isn't it?" said Parker. "I don't have to ask your permission to buy an ice-cream cone."

"Where's Jessica?" I asked. I hardly ever saw Jessica anymore, and when I did, she wasn't with Parker.

Parker didn't answer. She just walked away licking this double-scoop bubble-gum cone. We agreed on bubble gum as our favorite flavor the summer we were best friends, but I switched to pumpkin afterwards, on principle.

Anyway, whenever I got near the Ables' house, Parker would accidentally on purpose come around the corner, and I had to pretend I was going somewhere else. So we were into the middle of November before I had a chance to talk to Maud and Amory again. Even that was due to a stroke of spectacular good luck.

This is what happened. I thought it was going to be an awful day because first of all it was drizzling and I overslept, and when my mother came in to find out why, she found Ronald in my bed. I guess Ronald had been rolling in the dirt or something the day before because the sheets looked kind of gray in places. My mother got really mad and said Ronald had to be out of the house by the end of the week.

"It may be dirt, but at least it's clean dirt!" I told her. "Did you know that human bites are a million times more dangerous than dog bites? My skin may be clean, but inside I'm dirtier than Ronald."

"Come to think of it, your skin doesn't look too clean either," said my mother.

To make things worse, it was Monday. We always did math in school on Monday mornings, and I happened to know that this Monday there was going to be a quiz.

It turned out to be worse than I expected because it wasn't the usual kind of quiz, where you can take your time and look at the problems. Instead, we had to choose teams and take turns answering questions, kind of like a spelling bee.

I'm good at spelling, but everyone knows how bad I am in math. I was the last person picked, and the captain put me at the end of the line. The two teams were tied when the teacher got to me, and all the kids on my side were looking at me with these really hopeless faces, as if they knew ahead of time I would answer wrong.

The teacher was pretty nice, and she must have known how awful I felt because she gave me a really easy question. Ordinarily I could have answered it without even thinking, but somehow my mind went blank. I looked at all those faces, and there was this terrible buzzing sound in my ears.

"Come on, Martha!" said the captain of my team. "We haven't got all day, you know."

I was about to say something, not the right answer but just anything so I could sit down and get it over with, when the buzzing turned into a deafening ring. At first I thought it was only my ears, but the kids started squealing and lining up at the door, and I realized it was a fire alarm. I couldn't believe my luck!

We huddled together in the playground waiting for the bell to stop ringing so we could go back inside. All the kids were shivering because we didn't have time to grab our coats, and it was still drizzling and really cold. I don't know who got the crazy idea of having a fire drill on a day like that. It was probably a mistake, but I didn't care how long we stayed outside, because if we stayed long enough, it would be time for Spanish when we went back in.

So I stood there still kind of dazed at my good luck and hoping the bell would go on ringing forever when this big wet black thing flew at me and knocked me over. Literally knocked me over! It was Ronald Reagan.

You can imagine the commotion. Everybody in school knew who Ronald was and that she belonged to me. They all started laughing and screaming, so when the principal came out to tell us to go back inside, she couldn't get anyone's attention.

"Martha Albright, is that your dog?" she yelled at me.

I said yes it was. She asked me how Ronald got there, and I said I didn't know. She was supposed to be locked up in our kitchen. I found out later that my mother had come home to get a folder she forgot, and Ronald must have slipped out when she wasn't looking. But all I could think of at the time was that Ronald had learned my trick with the kitchen window.

Anyway, the principal gave me permission to take Ronald home and then come straight back to school. I was so afraid she would remember there was no one at home to let me in that I left right away, without going in for my coat. I put my belt through Ronald's collar for a leash, and I ran as fast as I could. But not toward home. This was my first chance in days to pay a visit to the Ables!

This time it was Maud who opened the door. She looked really upset when she saw me, but it wasn't because she wished I wasn't there. It was because I was drenched. She didn't ask any questions. She just said, "Oh, dear! Oh, dear!" over and over and trotted off to get a towel. In fact, she brought back two towels, one for Ronald and one for me. While I was drying Ronald, Maud kept rubbing my hair with the other towel and saying, "Oh, dear!"

"I'm all right," I said. "I won't catch cold, I promise," and I told her about the fire drill. "Isn't Mr. Able at home?" I asked.

"He's out in the kitchen, making lunch," said Maud. "Won't you stay for lunch?"

"I already ate," I told her. It was only eleven-thirty, but for all Maud knew, we ate early at school. I wasn't going to risk another banana-salami stew.

The minute I walked into the kitchen I recognized the smell. Amory Able had this frilly yellow apron, which must have belonged to Maud, tied around his waist, and he was just dropping in the lima beans. He glared at me and grunted, but I knew him well enough by then to know it was just his way of saying hello.

"You're in luck," he told me. "I'm making your favorite dish."

"I've *had* lunch," I said, crossing my fingers. "I'm stuffed."

"Then stir!" said Amory Able, motioning me over to the stove. "I have to go down to the cellar. I'm out of port wine."

While I stood there stirring, I thought how thankful I was that I had inherited Amory Able's love for dogs instead of his bossy disposition. No wonder Arabella ran away from home! He was fun to visit from time to time, but could you imagine living with someone like that? To say nothing of being raised on banana-salami stew!

I was daydreaming about Arabella and wondering if I could get them to show me a photograph when this loud voice yelled at me, "Watch what you're doing!"

I jumped a mile in the air and dropped the spoon.

"No use doing a job at all unless you intend to do it well," said Amory Able as he added a dollop of port wine.

I thought that was a little unfair. After all, he was the one who asked me to stir. "What did I do wrong?" I asked.

"You were stirring counterclockwise," said Amory Able.

"So what?" I asked. "I bet gourmet cooks stir any way they like!"

Amory Able rinsed the spoon and started stirring again, his way. "Gourmet cooking is poppycock!" he said. "Calvin Coolidge."

I was pretty sure Amory Able made that up himself, and I thought how lucky it was for Calvin Coolidge that he never said all the things Amory Able told me he did. I mean, who would vote for a president who always wanted to have the last word on everything? But I didn't want Amory Able to get started on Calvin Coolidge again, so I changed the subject.

"Tell me about Arabella," I said. "Did she look like me? Did she have green eyes?"

Maud put her head to one side and stared hard at me for a while as if she saw me for the first time. I thought maybe this was the moment when the Ables put two and two together. I could imagine Maud gathering me in her arms, the way they do in books, and saying, "It's like having our darling Arabella back again!"

But she didn't. She just said, "No, dear."

I was working up the nerve to ask whether Arabella ran away with a dog trainer when I suddenly had a terrific idea. I had just gotten a letter in the mail from my father. It was a private letter, not for sharing with my mother and Kermit. It was mostly nice, saying how much he missed riding with me on Sundays and trying to explain why Parker was being so stinky and what to do about it. But the end of the letter was awful. My father wrote how hard he knew it must have been for me to give up Ronald Reagan. I felt a little guilty and a little scared.

I couldn't bear to part with Ronald, but if she had to go, it wouldn't be so bad if she went someplace close. Maybe I could get the Ables to keep her for me!

I wanted time to think about it, though. Besides, it was getting on toward noon, which meant the kids were lining up to go to the cafeteria. I still had to go home and get Ronald back through that kitchen window.

"I ought to be getting back to school," I announced.

"That's the spirit!" said Amory Able. "Keep your nose to the grindstone. 'A child miseducated is a child lost.' Calvin Coolidge."

"School wasn't as bad as usual today," I said.

I told him about my fantastic luck getting out of the math quiz, but Amory Able didn't seem to appreciate it.

"Don't be a quitter," he said. "Do you know the poem about the quitter?"

"No," I said. "Robert Service?"

Right again. He quoted:

"But to fight and to fight when hope's out of sight—
Why, that's the best game of them all!"

He waved his fork around in the air like a lunatic
and took another bite of stew. I told him that if you fight
in our school, they send you to the principal's office,
which is a place I end up in often enough as it is. But I
didn't want him to get the idea I was a dumb student or
something.

"I get good grades in most subjects," I told him.
"It's only in math that hope's out of sight. If I could
change the world, I'd have a law saying no math until
college."

For all I know I'll be dead by the time I'm that old,
but even if I'm still alive, at least I will have enjoyed my
childhood.

Amory Able didn't look as if he agreed with me, but
Maud nodded and asked what else I would change. It
was about time somebody asked me that question! I had
this list made, just in case.

"Every child could have a dog," I said, "and there'd
be no more pollution. I'd have cows lay eggs, to econ-
omize on chickens, and the government would give more
money to orphans. I'd have the president put an amend-
ment in the constitution saying it's okay for girls to go in
the boys' room. And if I could really change whatever I
wanted, I'd want the earth to have a couple more
moons."

Amory Able said that if I got the price of a loaf of
bread back down to a nickel, my list would be just about
perfect. Then Maud piped up and asked if I wouldn't

mind bringing back the streetcars while I was at it. I said sure, that was okay with me.

"Thank you, dear," she said. "Georgetown was so much nicer when the streetcars were running. I used to take Arabella for rides when she was a baby, and she would laugh and laugh when the driver rang the bell."

I was hoping I could get them back on the subject of Arabella, but Amory Able slammed his fork down on the table. "Poppycock! Those old trolleys never had bells."

"Indeed they did, dear," said Maud. "I remember distinctly. If they hadn't had bells, there would have been no point in taking Arabella for the ride."

I could see she thought this clinched the argument, but Amory Able just repeated, "Poppycock!"

Maud's face turned pink. "You're wrong, dear," she said, "but it's not worth discussing. Streetcars are gone forever, bells or not."

"There were no bells!" Amory Able shouted. "Let's get that straight, once and for all!"

Then he calmed down and scowled at me. "You'll find in life that if a woman gets one thing wrong, she tends to get a whole slew of other things wrong too," he said. "Stands to reason."

Ronald stood up and shook herself, and I realized how late it was getting. I started backing out of the room. "You're probably right," I said.

When I reached the front door, I could still hear Maud's voice squeaking about the trolley bells, and then Amory Able roared out, "Once you've raised your voice, you've lost the argument! Calvin Coolidge!"

I closed the door behind me and hurried back home.

It was no easy business shoving Ronald Reagan through that kitchen window, but I finally managed it. When I got back to school, no one said a thing about how long I had been gone. We had science that afternoon, which wasn't so bad, especially when Carlos Lopez dropped the dry ice down Michelle MacPherson's collar and Michelle had hysterics.

The rain kept up, so we couldn't play kickball at Saint Michael's after school. To make things better, Sondra had a headache, so instead of playing bingo or expressing our personalities with our bottoms, we got to read books.

I asked Larry if he was going to make us all read the same book, but he said not to be facetious. I looked up facetious in the dictionary. It means trying to be funny at the inappropriate time. I don't see what's so funny about sticking up for my rights at Saint Michael's, which is so undemocratic, in spite of what my mother says, that someday it's going to make a big scandal in the newspapers.

Anyway, it turned out to be a fairly good day, and for once I came home in a fairly good mood. My mother even commented on it when she coached me in math that evening.

"It's nice to see you looking so happy, Martha!" she said. "Are things going better for you at school?"

"Sure," I said. " 'A child miseducated is a child lost.' Calvin Coolidge."

"Wrong president," my mother corrected me. "John F. Kennedy said that. What's this sudden obsession with Calvin Coolidge?"

"Never mind," I said. I didn't want to give her the wrong impression about the person who might be the answer to my problem with Ronald.

First, I had to persuade Amory Able to take Ronald in case of an emergency, which I prayed would never happen. Then I had to track down Arabella. I was sure her parents would forgive her for running away, and with luck they would forgive my dog-trainer father too.

I imagined this wonderful scene where Maud gathers her daughter into her arms, where Amory shakes hands with the dog trainer, and where they all tell me how grateful they are. Then I step forward and tell them I'm their long-lost baby girl. There would be a lot of tears and stuff, and of course they would say I could keep Ronald forever.

But how would I go about tracking down Arabella? I had a feeling it might not be too easy. I thought about it for a long time, and it struck me that there was only one way to do it.

Advertise!

# Chapter 6

Obviously I couldn't put ads in newspapers all over the country. From my experience with the ad about Ronald, I knew that each word costs money, sort of like a telegram. Money I simply didn't have.

I could start saving my allowance, but my allowance wouldn't go far if I put regular ads in the dailies. Instead, I decided to put one in *The Georgetowner*, which is a local paper that comes out every two weeks and tells what goes on in the neighborhood. A lot of people read it, and since Arabella grew up in Georgetown, there was a chance some reader was still in touch with her and would notice my ad, which I planned very carefully.

> ARABELLA: *Come back! All is*
> *forgiven! But first call 905-*
> *1713 after school or weekends*

I didn't put in my name because it would have gone into the next line, which costs another dollar, and as it was, I was completely broke. I have a sweet tooth, so my allowance lasts only until the middle of the week. That may be a good thing because if I were any richer, I'd be a lot fatter too.

The problem was that this ad was costing me three dollars, plus the stamp, and that meant close to a month's allowance, if I resisted my sweet tooth. But if I waited a month, it might be too late!

A lot of the kids in our neighborhood earn money by raking leaves or shoveling snow off peoples' sidewalks, but the leaves had finished falling and the snow hadn't started yet. I was too young to baby-sit or get a job at the ice-cream parlor. How was I going to get rich fast? I was so desperate that I ended up asking Amory Able for advice.

Amory Able was in an unusually good mood when I talked to him, and he gave my problem his full attention. He quoted:

> "It's bully in a high-toned joint to eat and drink
> your fill,
> But it's quite another matter when you
> Pay the bill.

"Robert Service," he said.

I told him I always paid cash down for my shakes and sundaes, which was why I needed more money now.

Amory Able then quoted:

> "I wanted the gold, and I got it—
> Came out with a fortune last fall,—

> Yet somehow life's not what I thought it,
>    And somehow the gold isn't all."

"Robert Service," I added automatically. I wondered whether Amory Able was referring to himself. If so, it was too bad he had so much money and didn't care about it when all I needed was three dollars and a twenty-cent stamp. I considered asking him for a loan, but somehow I didn't have the nerve.

"How did you make your fortune?" I asked.

Amory Able told me he had no fortune, not to speak of. He said the only people nowadays making fortunes were the people who sell you a loaf of bread for a dollar forty-nine.

"When I was a boy, it was easy enough to pick up a nickel here and there," he said. "Back then a nickel would get you into the movies."

I asked him how he earned his nickel. "Shining shoes," he told me, "or selling lemonade."

That gave me two ideas to start with, and I decided to try the shoeshine business first because we had all the equipment.

People in our neighborhood are kind of informal, and they mostly wear joggers, but on Sunday a lot of them get dolled up to go to church. So the next Sunday I took all the shoe polish I could find and set up a big sign on the steps of Saint Michael's Church.

SHOESHINE!!
*Only Fifty Cents!*
*Praise the Lord with Clean Feet!*

I know fifty cents was a little steep, but I figured that if only seven people had a guilty conscience when they read about the Lord, I would have enough for my ad and the stamp plus a Hershey bar to celebrate.

But the people going into Saint Michael's that day must have had no conscience at all, although some of them certainly had dirty shoes. Not one single person asked for a shine, even when I crossed out fifty and wrote five.

In fact, one man came up and asked me why I wasn't in Sunday school with the rest of the kids. I told him I put in fifteen hours a week at Saint Michael's as it was, so I deserved a vacation on Sundays.

The man said in that case I should pack up and go home to my parents, which I think shows a total absence of Christian spirit. And you should have seen his shoes: filthy! I offered him a free shine, just to turn the other cheek, but he said it would make him late for church.

Well, there obviously wasn't any money in the shoe-shine business, so I went home and set up a lemonade stand instead, out on our front steps.

We had only two cans of frozen lemonade, so I had to add some tomato juice. Then I made another sign.

> ICE-COLD PINK LEMONADE!!
> *Only Fifty Cents!*
> *Last Chance for a Drink*
> *Before Wisconsin Avenue!*

That happened to be true. No one else was selling lemonade that afternoon because it had begun to rain, and the temperature had dropped down to forty.

People went by, but nobody even looked at my sign. I thought maybe they couldn't see from under their umbrellas, so whenever anyone came I would scream, "Ice-cold lemonade! Only fifty cents!"

My mother came out to see what all the hollering was about, and she was annoyed. She told me: one, it was too cold to be out without a jacket; two, nobody in their right mind would drink ice-cold anything in the freezing rain; and, three, no daughter of hers was going to charge fifty cents for a Dixie cup of lemonade.

"Why do you keep pretending I'm your daughter?" I asked.

I guess I went a little too far for once because my mother started shouting. I won't go into everything she said, but the part that really got me was that I either had to pay for the cans of juice or else I had to drink pink lemonade at meals until it was all gone.

I didn't need any more expenses, so I drank. And I found out it isn't such a good idea to mix tomato juice with lemonade, even though they both taste fine by themselves.

Well, the weather got colder and wetter day by day, and to make things worse, all of a sudden we were in the middle of Thanksgiving vacation. Although we were out of school all week, my mother got off work for only one day. That meant four full days of Saint Michael's, from nine to six. It was enough to drive anyone up the wall, and believe me, the whole group went a little crazy.

It rained every single day that week, although by rights we should have been having a spell of Indian summer. So every day we were cooped up in that dumb community room, every day we had a double dose of bingo, and every single day we had to express our personalities.

On the last day Sondra even asked us to bring leotards so we would look like real dancers. I don't happen to own a leotard, so I had to wear my bathing suit instead. My bathing suit is yellow with green frogs all over it. But the Rodriguez twins had matching tutus with ruffles on the seat and spangles on the chest. Did they ever look stupid!

My mother was kind of sad around then because my father couldn't be home for Thanksgiving, and that had never happened before. Most families get together with grandparents or other relatives, but my grandparents live out on the West Coast, and if we get together at all, it's during summer vacation.

But a few days before Thanksgiving my mother came home from work looking more cheerful and said she had had this great idea. "I think we should *share* Thanksgiving this year," she said. "We should show that we're grateful for the happy lives we lead, even though Daddy can't be home this year."

I could have said a thing or two about happy lives, but I didn't want to make her feel guilty. "Who are we going to share with?" I asked.

My mother said we should invite someone who would be alone on Thanksgiving. "I was thinking of old Mrs. McGrath down the street," she said, "and we could have Mr. Purse as well."

Now, I've already said how I feel about Christian spirit, but this was going too far. Mrs. McGrath hates kids, and she yells at me and Kermit when we bicycle on the sidewalk. As for Mr. Purse, he's the man whose car smashed into that pick-up truck when Ronald Reagan was jaywalking.

"I bet I could find somebody lonelier than that," I told her.

My mother asked who, for instance, and I said how about my teacher. I had this idea that teachers don't have any friends in real life due to their bossy dispositions, but it turned out I was wrong. When I asked Ms. Folan the next day, she said she had a husband and five children, and her mother-in-law lived with them too.

That night my mother was reaching for the phone to call Mr. Purse, and I was feeling pretty desperate. I didn't think I could give thanks for anything if I were sitting across the table from someone who hated Ronald. So all of a sudden I said, "Wait! I know this old couple in a house up on Dent Place, and they're *really* lonely!"

My mother put down the receiver and asked me to tell her more about them. So I told her that the Ables were these old people I was friends with, and I happened to know they were really unhappy since their daughter ran away from home with a dog trainer, and they hadn't a friend in the world except for me.

"They're really nice!" I said. "That is, *he's* a little cuckoo, but underneath he's just as nice as she is. He's teaching me how to cook."

My mother looked at me suspiciously. "Is this the old couple you once tried to convince me were your grandparents? You must be wearing them to the bone!"

"I haven't broken the good news to them yet," I reassured her. "I haven't got enough proof. How can I if you won't cooperate?"

My mother sighed, but she said I could invite the Ables.

"Maybe you could cook something for our meal," she suggested. "That would show Mr. Able that you're grateful for his lessons."

I told her that so far he had given me only one lesson, so I didn't know how to make anything yet. I couldn't see banana-salami stew on my mother's plate along with sweet potatoes and cranberry sauce.

Well, I ran up to Dent Place and asked the Ables if they could come, and they said yes, they would be delighted. Maud turned pink, and Amory grunted and cleared his throat. I was afraid he was going to come up with some Calvin Coolidge for the occasion, so I said I had to run home and help my mother cook since Thanksgiving was the next day.

The Ables turned up at one o'clock sharp. None of this fashionable fifteen-minutes-late business for them. Maud was dressed in a frilly polka-dot silk affair, and it looked as if she had had her hair done. Amory wore this dark blue pin-striped double-breasted suit that I had never seen him in, and he carried a cane.

I felt as if they were strangers, and the Ables must have felt the same about me because I guess it was the first time they had ever seen me in a dress and party shoes. I detest party shoes. Ronald must have hated them too because the minute I put them on, she hid under my bed and wouldn't come out, in spite of the good smells coming from the kitchen.

My mother was a little formal when she met the Ables, but Kermit took to them right away, even though

Amory Able kept calling him "young man." Maud embarrassed me by asking why I hadn't ever brought my darling little brother to visit them. I began to wonder if I had been right to introduce them to my family so soon, but after my mother got the food on the table, things went better.

My mother sat with Mr. Able on her left and Maud on her right. I sat next to Amory, and Kermit sat next to Maud. The place at the end of the table was empty, which made me keep thinking about my father. Real father or not, I would have given six months' allowance to have him sitting there just then. Once I had paid for the ad about Arabella, that is.

Well, the first thing that happened was that my mother asked Amory Able to say grace. I was afraid he would mind, but on the contrary, he got that smug look on his face again, and I could guess what was coming.

He bowed his head and chanted:

> "It's a might good world, so it is, dear lass,
> When even the worst is said.
> There's a smile and a tear, a sigh and a cheer,
> But better be living than dead."

My mother raised her eyebrows. "Is that a prayer?" she asked.

I told her it was Robert Service. "But it's nowhere near as good as 'Lipstick Liz'," I said. "Could you recite 'Lipstick Liz' for my mother, Mr. Able?"

Amory Able glared at me and said it would be inappropriate for the occasion.

Well, as I said, once we got the turkey on the table,

things began to liven up. First of all, Amory Able insisted on cutting up the bird. My mother didn't mind, but she looked a little put out when he did it with his penknife, especially after he told her that women don't know how to get a good edge on a kitchen knife. My mother doesn't appreciate remarks about women.

Kermit asked if he could use the knife to cut a piece of bread, and Amory Able handed it to him saying, "Whittle from and you'll never cut you! Calvin Coolidge."

Kermit looked Amory Able straight in the eye and asked, "What the hell is Calvin Coolidge?"

For a moment I thought Amory Able was going to choke. His face got red, and he thumped the floor with his cane and glared at Kermit. I could see my mother was going to get at Kermit for swearing, but just then Maud started to giggle, and she giggled harder and harder until I thought she would have hysterics.

My mother obviously didn't see what was so funny. She frowned at Kermit, who was whittling from, and she said, "That's French bread, Kermit. It doesn't need to be cut. Just break off a piece and give the knife back to Mr. Able."

"French bread, eh?" said Amory Able. "I don't hold with your namby-pamby French cooking." Whereupon Maud stopped giggling and looked down at her sweet potatoes in a pained sort of way.

"Can't understand why people are attracted to all this fancy French-style food when you can get better quality for a quarter of the price if you have the gumption to do without the gewgaws," Amory Able went on. "Don't know what you pay for a loaf of French bread nowadays, but when I was a boy, you could buy a loaf of bread for a nickel. Even now you can dine off a can of sardines for only ninety-three cents."

My mother said she preferred turkey at Thanksgiving, and she passed the platter. Amory Able helped himself to the drumstick, and there was this embarrassing silence while he chewed. Then Maud started telling my mother how lucky she was to have such attractive, healthy children. That was a little embarrassing too, but it was better than silence.

As soon as Amory Able polished off the first drumstick, I handed him the other. I figured it was safer to keep his mouth full. I kept an eye on him to make sure he didn't suddenly swallow and start misquoting Calvin Coolidge again, but my attention was mostly on Maud's conversation with my mother.

"—and Martha has such lovely coloring with those pretty hazel eyes!" Maud was saying.

Hazel? That sounded a lot nicer than green. I began to listen harder.

"She must have been a darling baby!" said Maud. "I would simply love to see some early photographs, if it isn't an imposition."

I knew what was coming. My mother got the same old, innocent expression on her face and said she was sorry, but she didn't have a single picture of me before I was two years old.

"None at all?" asked Maud. "What a pity! I know young parents are often too busy to think of it, but photographs are such a blessing when a child grows up and leaves home!"

"Oh, we *took* plenty of photographs," my mother

said. "We must have taken hundreds! But one of our suitcases was lost the year we moved from Brussels to Paris, and all of Martha's baby pictures happened to be inside."

Happened! Just happened! How could she have the nerve to keep on telling people a story like that? I was dying to make her confess the truth right then and there. It was time for a showdown. So I took a deep breath and was about to begin, but unfortunately Kermit whittled to and cut his finger. There was blood all over the French bread, and I could just hear Calvin Coolidge saying, "I told you so!"

It wasn't such a bad cut, but Kermit gets upset if he sees even the tiniest drop of blood, so my mother had to take him out to the kitchen to patch him up, and Amory Able went too. There she was, holding Kermit's finger under running water and trying to convince him he wasn't dying, and all the while Amory Able waved around the top part of our double boiler and talked a mile a minute.

"I hope you're not one of these women who never tightens the screws on your pot handles!" he told her, and just then the pot fell off its handle and crashed down on the kitchen floor.

My mother screamed and Kermit started to cry. "Mr. Able!" I called from the dining room. "You haven't finished your drumstick! You don't want it to go to waste, do you?"

That got him out of the kitchen. He came back, pulling this big white handkerchief out of his pocket. Before I could say anything, he reached for that drumstick and wrapped it up. In his handkerchief!

"I'll use it in my stew," he explained. "Ought to add a nice flavor."

"Don't you want me to wrap it in foil?" I asked. "It's awfully greasy!"

But just then my mother brought in the apple pie. So we sat down again, and Amory Able put the handkerchief with the drumstick wrapped up inside it in his pocket.

Nobody talked for a long time. Kermit was pale, and Maud Able was blushing, and my mother was a trifle frazzled. I sat there listening to them all chew. I was so full of turkey that I wasn't hungry for pie, even though after apple there was pumpkin, which is my favorite.

It seemed to me that the meal was dragging, but just as I was beginning to think it would last forever, the phone rang.

I felt as if the sun had come out after a storm because it was my father, calling from South America.

Except for letters, we hadn't heard from my father since he left home in September, so the whole family went wild. My mother talked for hours, and after that Kermit and I got a turn. Then my mother grabbed the phone and talked some more. Even Ronald came skittering downstairs, barking like crazy.

The Amorys just sat at the table and looked polite. At least, Maud looked polite. Mr. Able looked bored, so I thought maybe it was a good time to get him used to the idea of having Ronald come to stay. I sat down next to him and started scratching Ronald's ears.

"It sure is nice to have a dog, isn't it, Mr. Able?" I asked.

Ronald loves having her ears scratched. The only

problem is that it makes her drool. But I mopped up the drool with my napkin as fast as it came out.

Amory Able grunted. "People who can't bother to train a dog properly shouldn't be allowed to keep one," he said. "Dog's place is in the yard, not at the table."

Ordinarily I would have disagreed with that, but I made a big effort to keep my temper.

"I bet you're really good at training dogs," I said. "It's too bad you weren't around when they were training Ronald."

Amory Able grunted again. He looked kind of pleased. "Not a bad animal, basically," he said. "Just needs a firm hand. Nothing a week or so of discipline wouldn't cure."

I was just about to make arrangements for taking Ronald to him for a week or so of discipline if my mother ever got around to calling the pound, when Ronald spoiled everything.

I guess she could tell that Amory Able was saying something nice about her, so she went and put her head on his lap. And then wouldn't you know it, she must have smelled the turkey because she snapped that drumstick out of Amory Able's pocket and started chewing it up, handkerchief and all.

I'm afraid that was the end of what wasn't a very pleasant afternoon to begin with. Amory Able got all red in the face and waved his cane around, and Maud Able stood up in a hurry.

My mother hung up the phone and came running over. "You're not leaving yet, I hope!" she said. "How about some coffee?"

"Never touch coffee!" said Amory Able. "Sure way to curdle your guts."

"I don't like to contradict, dear!" Maud began.

"Then don't!" said Amory.

"—but I read in the paper that coffee aids in the digestive process!" Maud squeaked.

"Poppycock!" roared Amory Able.

He stamped out of the house, and Maud scuttled after him, smiling at me and my mother in this apologetic way.

"Well!" said my mother. "What got into *him*?"

I wasn't going to say anything, but Kermit had to go and tell her what happened, so she got all upset.

"That does it!" she said. "Ronald has to be out of here by this time tomorrow. Your father was horrified to hear her barking. I'm calling the pound in the morning!"

"Don't!" I cried. "Please don't! I'll find a place for her to stay, I promise!"

My mother got that worried look in her eyes again, so I went off to the kitchen and started stacking up the plates. It's a wonder I didn't break any. I was crying so hard that I could hardly see what I was doing. After what happened that afternoon, Amory Able would never agree to take Ronald, and if I lost Ronald, life just wouldn't be worth living.

# Chapter 7

I slept badly that night, and I guess I must have looked pretty miserable the next morning because my mother took pity on me, at last.

"Listen, sweetie," she said. "I wasn't serious about sending Ronald to the pound. I wouldn't have the heart to do that any more than you would. The problem is, your father is right. Our family moves around too much to have a dog. We're going to have to find another home for Ronald sooner or later, and the longer we wait, the more it's going to hurt."

"You said all that before," I reminded her. "It was weeks ago, and Ronald is still here and everything is going fine. She's a whole lot happier than she was when we found her, and so am I, so why can't we keep on keeping her?"

My mother just sighed.

"Stop worrying about it!" I said. "I'll work something out, I promise! Just give me time."

Time! Since Thanksgiving was on the twenty-sixth

that year, there were only four more days until December. Time was going by so fast that if I didn't get moving, I would reach majority before I had my own dog.

I wanted that ad about Arabella to get to *The Georgetowner* in time for their next issue, but I was still one hundred percent stone broke. In fact, I owed thirty-four cents to Kermit for a popsicle I bought back in August, and he was beginning to talk about charging interest.

I had to be at Saint Michael's all day Friday, of course, which was the day I expressed my personality in a yellow bathing suit with green frogs. Thank goodness it was the end of the week! At least I had two days in front of me to overcome my humiliation.

But on Saturday I had a stroke of luck. My mother sent me to the drugstore after breakfast to buy the paper and a quart of milk. While I was in there, I noticed this sign pinned up to the bulletin board:

WANTED!!
*Responsible person to*
*walk large sheep dog.*

At the bottom of the page were slips of paper with a telephone number that you could tear off if you were interested.

Naturally I was interested, and just as I was about to tear off a slip, this big grubby hand reached up and grabbed one first. Not that it mattered because there were plenty more, but if there's one thing I can't stand, it's pushy people. So I spun around to say what I thought about it, and guess who it was?

"Copy cat!" I said.

Parker answered back, "This is a free country, isn't it?"

She made a dash for the door. I could tell she was trying to get home to the phone before me, but I had to pay for the milk and paper before I left the store.

There was a long line, and the girl at the cash register ran out of nickels and had to go get more, so I knew there was no hope of calling first about the sheep dog. But when it was finally my turn, the girl handed me fifteen cents change, and I had a brain wave. I didn't need to go home to call. I could call right there from the public phone!

My hands were shaking when I dialed the number. I was afraid it would be busy—a sure sign that Parker had gotten there first—but I was lucky for once. An old lady answered. At least she sounded like an old lady, and she said to come right over—her dog needed exercise—and if it worked out, I would get the job. Believe me, I ran.

Of course first I had to take home the milk and the paper, and it took a couple of minutes to persuade Kermit to lend me fifteen more cents to pay my mother back for the phone call. Kermit said that made forty-nine cents, which would come to fifty-three point nine at ten percent interest if I didn't pay him back by Christmas Eve. Sometimes I think Kermit only learns math so he can persecute his sister.

Just as I was about to leave the house again, my mother said I had to take Ronald along too. "This is the first time you've ever wanted to leave her behind," she said when I objected. "And by the way, what have you done about finding her a new home?"

Then she started wondering why no one ever answered that ad in the paper, so I grabbed Ronald's rope and left the house fast.

I didn't think it would make too big a hit if I turned up with a dog of my own, especially one like Ronald, who doesn't always behave like a civilized human being. So when I reached the address the old lady gave me, I tied Ronald to a lamppost across the street. Then I rang the bell.

I thought she sounded like an old lady over the phone, but I had no idea she would be as old as all that. She looked like a bag of bones, and I was afraid that if I sneezed, I would knock her over. No wonder she needed someone to walk her dog!

When I met the dog, the first thing I thought was how the sign was a little misleading. I mean, it said, "Large Sheep Dog." This may or may not have been a sheep dog. I'm not too good about breeds because most of the dogs I know are no breed at all. But "large" was downright dishonest. It was *enormous*!

How that lady had lived to a ripe old age with a monster that could send her sky high with one wag of its tail was beyond me. It must have weighed six times as much as I did, and I had to stand on tiptoe to look it in the eye. Or so it seemed at the time.

"What's his name?" I asked.

The old lady said, "Buttercup."

I must say one thing: Buttercup was friendly. She took to me right off, which almost ruined my chances of getting the job because when she licked my face, she knocked me down. The old lady looked doubtful, and she said she didn't think I was strong enough to walk Buttercup.

"I've had a lot of experience," I said. "I got a masters degree in dog-walking at Georgetown University."

This wasn't true, although I hoped it might be one day. But I said it anyway because I needed money really badly.

The old lady said I looked too young to be in college, and I said yes I was, by a year or so, but this wasn't college. This was Continuing Education.

I could see she was still thinking of a polite way to say no, and I was about to give up when I looked out the window and saw Parker on the sidewalk, staring at the house.

"United we stand and divided we fall!" I said to myself. That isn't Calvin Coolidge. It's something out of my social studies book.

"I have a friend helping me," I told the old lady. "We won't have any trouble with Buttercup if we're both holding on to her leash. And we can give you references. We walk dogs for three senators and a movie star."

I promised myself I would go to church that week to make up for all the stories I was telling.

Luckily the old lady didn't ask for references because forgery wasn't really in my line. Instead, she said, "Well, I suppose there's no harm in trying. If you're sure your friend will help."

She stood in her doorway watching as I took Buttercup out of the house, so I had to let Parker in on the secret. "I don't get the job unless you come along too," I hissed at her.

Parker looked suspicious.

"We'll neither of us get it by ourselves," I said. "Come on, I'll share the pay."

"How much is she paying us?" Parker asked. She took hold of Buttercup's collar and turned to wave at the old lady to show it was okay.

The old lady seemed satisfied and went back into her house. It was a good thing she did because that way she didn't see what happened when Buttercup met Ronald Reagan.

I mean it was nothing bad—they got along fine—but somehow each seemed to encourage the bounciness in the other. It took a while to get their leashes untangled because they were rolling around and play-biting at each other, and we were afraid of getting hurt. When we finally got them straightened out, we made a deal. First I would walk Buttercup, and Parker would walk Ronald, and then we would switch.

Well, it took exactly one minute to find out *that* wouldn't work, but thank goodness we were already around the corner. What happened was that Ronald and Buttercup decided they would rather walk each other. They kept crossing back and forth until their leashes got all tangled together again. Then just as Parker and I were unraveling them, they dashed off in different directions after two squirrels. It took us five minutes to catch the dogs, and I skinned my right knee.

After that we decided to let Ronald loose and concentrate our strength on Buttercup. So we undid Ronald's rope and tied it to Buttercup's collar, and I held the rope and Parker held the leash. We headed for the Georgetown University campus, where the students tend to be nicer about dogs than our neighbors. But even there things didn't go so well.

At first Ronald trotted along with us so nicely that anyone who didn't know her might think she had been taught to heel. Buttercup was pretty good too, though she kept accidentally knocking over all the trash baskets.

Parker and I weren't paying too much attention because we were arguing about how to split up the pay. I thought I should get ninety percent because I landed the job, but Parker said I never would have been hired except for her, so it should be fifty-fifty. It didn't make things easier not to know what the pay was going to be, but I figured it ought to be at least ten dollars an hour, taking account of Buttercup's size.

Well, the discussion was getting a little heated, so we didn't notice when this bicycle came by. Ronald has a thing about bicycles. It's probably because they don't stop to sniff the way other dogs do. They just go zipping by, which is considered really bad manners among dogs. So Ronald feels she ought to teach the bicycle a lesson, and she sometimes misses and gets the rider instead.

Ronald only got the cuff of the man's pants, so I didn't see what he had to complain about, but complain he did. Buttercup was curious and started pulling on her leash. Leashes, I should say. And just then this little black poodle came dashing over, dragging a silly-looking lady in a white tennis outfit after it. The poodle took a violent dislike to Buttercup, who was mad at the man on the bike for being mean to Ronald, and Ronald was still trying to teach the bike a lesson. It was an awkward situation.

Parker and I pulled Buttercup's leashes as hard as

we could. Unfortunately we didn't notice that the rope was wound around the tennis-lady's leg. We ended up pulling her over, and Buttercup kind of collapsed on top of her. The incident was on the noisy side, and a lot of people started crowding around and giving advice, so before we knew it, the campus police turned up.

I must admit that the Georgetown campus police are pretty efficient. Before I even had time to explain, the dogs were separated, and the man on the bike was off to some class he said he was late for. The lady with the poodle walked away in a huff carrying her poodle, who I happen to know didn't even get scratched. That left just me and Parker and Ronald and Buttercup.

The campus policeman asked who was responsible for the two dogs. I looked around for Parker, but she had disappeared. Parker is a real expert at disappearing.

The policeman was nice when I explained about my new job, but he insisted on walking me back to the old lady's house. After he got through talking to her, she took Buttercup inside and locked the door. I didn't get paid at all, not so much as a nickel, which won't even buy a Hershey bar nowadays, to say nothing of a loaf of bread.

As I said, that was the last Saturday in November. We had just one day left of vacation, and when I got home from dog-walking, I found Kermit in the middle of this big discussion with my mother.

Kermit was saying it wasn't fair that I got to invite the Ables for Thanksgiving dinner when he hadn't had a friend over for weeks. He kept asking my mother if he could have someone for the night, and my mother was wearing her face that means, "I'll go crazy if I don't get some peace and quiet, but I want to be a good parent."

"All right," she said, "but it has to be somebody quiet."

This narrowed Kermit's choice down to exactly zero, but it didn't seem to bother him. He went off whooping like a wild Indian, and when he came back from the phone, he looked as happy as the day his tent caterpillars came out of their tent.

"She can come!" Kermit shouted.

"She?" my mother repeated. "A girl? That's nice!"

I could see she wasn't really so sure it was nice, but then she remembered about equal rights and all that jazz that we hadn't heard about recently because she brings it up only when my father is at home.

"Who's your girlfriend?" I asked Kermit, and he answered, "Parker."

Parker in my house as my little brother's guest? "That's fine!" I said. "That's just dandy! And she can have my room because as it happens I'm not going to be here."

My mother asked me why not, and I said I was invited to spend the night with the Rodriguez twins. I thought they would be crazy to have me over, but when I called their number, all I got was this person speaking Spanish. At least I guess it was Spanish. So far all I can do in Spanish is count and say what color socks I'm wearing, plus the word for mushroom, which I had to learn for the Christmas play.

I hung up and ran all the way to Dent Place to see if I could wangle an invitation out of the Ables, but they weren't at home. They were out all day, and when it got dark, I had to admit to myself that maybe it wasn't true

I was their only friend in the world, so I went home.

Parker spent the whole evening in Kermit's room with the door closed. By the sounds coming out, I could tell they were playing with Kermit's locomotives. I yelled through the door when Kermit's favorite show was on TV, but they were having such a good time that he didn't want to come out. I told my mother I didn't think Parker was a suitable friend for Kermit. I told her for all she knew they were playing doctor, but she just smiled.

I thought Parker would go home on Sunday morning. I mean, her parents go to church every week, and after that her father drives them all out to the country for a walk. But my mother asked her if she could stay.

"There's an exhibit I'm dying to see," she explained. "If I knew there were three of you keeping tabs on each other, I'd feel better about leaving you alone."

I told my mother I would be perfectly safe with Ronald. "Why can't Kermit go over to Parker's house?" I asked. "Hasn't Parker been sponging off us long enough?"

"Thanks anyway," said Kermit. "We're building a tunnel through Mount Everest. It's going to take our railroad crew at least six months, so we're staying here today."

This is the kind of talk my mother thinks is really cute. It makes me sick, and I told Kermit so. But my mother said that if Kermit and Parker were happy, I should be happy too because that way I could be alone with Ronald.

So my mother went off to her exhibit, and Parker went to Kermit's room and locked the door. I just sat in the kitchen feeling Ronald Reagan for ticks. She didn't have a single one, so it wasn't a very exciting job.

I was just making up my mind to run Ronald over to the Ables, even though my mother made us promise not to leave the house, when Kermit and Parker burst into the kitchen saying they were starved.

"We need supplies!" Kermit told me. "Our men are starving. What's in the fridge?"

"Cold turkey," I said. We had been eating cold turkey until it was coming out of our ears.

"We need something more nutritious," said Kermit. "The snow and ice are demoralizing our crew. Aren't there any Hershey bars?"

I said of course there weren't. The only time we have really good stuff around the house is just after Halloween, and it goes so fast that I suspect my mother throws most of it away. Or come to think of it maybe she eats it herself after we go to bed. Knowing my mother's sweet tooth, I wouldn't put it past her.

"We need Hershey bars," said Kermit stubbornly. "Why don't you go buy some? I promise I won't tell if you share with Parker and me."

I told him I was stone broke, and Parker said she was too.

"I'm not," said Kermit. "Martha owes me forty-nine cents, but I can't get her to pay me back. One of these days I'm going to sue."

He sure was being smart-alecky that day. I guess having a big kid spend the night was going to his head.

Anyway, we took out the last of the pumpkin pie and split it three ways. While we were eating, we got to talking about how broke we were. Parker told Kermit about walking Buttercup, and I told Parker about shining shoes and selling lemonade. Kermit mushed his pie around with his fork and reminded us that there were only twenty-six more days until Christmas.

We have this uncle out in California who sends us money for Christmas, and I happen to know that Parker's grandparents always slip a ten-dollar bill into her stocking, even though after that they give her something big like skates.

It was nice to think about, but it wasn't buying any Hershey bars. "I can't wait until Christmas," I announced. "I need money right now."

I looked around me without thinking and said sort of casually, "It's too bad we can't sell some of the junk in this house, but I guess nobody would be crazy enough to buy it."

Parker had finished her pie, and she was picking at Kermit's. She must have been pretty hungry because after Kermit gets through playing with his food, it looks disgusting.

"People will buy anything if you make it cheap enough," Parker said. "My mom had this tag sale in our backyard one time, and everything was sold by the end of the day."

The three of us looked up at the same time, and I guess we all had the same look in our eyes. Translated, it came down to one word: MONEY!

# Chapter
# 8

I know my mother said not to go outside until she got back from the exhibit, but my own front steps is hardly what I would call outside. I set up a card table, and Parker printed a big poster.

TAG SALE!!!
*Top Quality Merchandise*
*Dirt Cheap!!*

"Merchandise" was Parker's word. She said it gave a professional touch, and she looked up the spelling in the dictionary. We wanted to put another sign down the block, but I was afraid my mother would see it on her way home. Down the block is outside, no matter how you look at it.

We started getting a few customers right away, although mostly it was kids who didn't have enough money to buy anything. So what we did was sell our old toys to the kids dirt cheap and made up for it by charging more for the stuff the grownups were interested in.

I got five dollars for the French omelette pan my mother never uses, and a dollar-fifty apiece for about twenty ashtrays. We have too many ashtrays in our house for a family where nobody smokes, but I got rid of only the crystal ones because all the others Kermit and I had made in school when we were little. I knew my mother felt kind of sentimental about them.

Kermit put a ten-dollar price tag on his bedside lamp. I didn't think anybody would pay that much, and besides, I didn't think Kermit ought to sell it. But Kermit said he always uses a flashlight anyway.

It was amazing what people were willing to buy! For instance, my party shoes were so awful that when my mother gave them to me, I said I wouldn't wear them if she paid me, but some lady came by and paid three-fifty for them!

Then I brought out this set of leather-bound books I know my father hates because once he got my mother to admit that she never read them, that she only kept them for snob appeal. A lot of people were interested in the books, but we didn't sell any because a neighbor came over from across the street and said they were too valuable.

"What's the point of selling them if they're not valuable?" I argued. "We need money!"

"Does your mother know you're doing this?" the neighbor asked.

I didn't feel like answering, so I took the books back inside and found some old Nancy Drews instead.

"We're not getting enough customers," said Parker when I came out again. "We need more publicity. Let's put up a sign at the corner."

"We said we wouldn't leave the house," I reminded her.

"It's not as if you were crossing the street or anything," said Parker. "Come on, I'll go with you and help."

So we made a second sign and went off with some tape and string to find a good place to put it. It took longer than I thought, and when we got back, there were about twenty people around the card table.

"How do you suppose Kermit got so many customers?" I wondered.

I soon found out. While Parker and I were gone, Kermit had brought out a few more things that he thought my mother would be glad to get rid of. First there were our demitasse spoons that my mother refuses to use because she says they look dinky. But still, they're silver. Then there was this Chinese vase from the table in the landing. My mother always says she knows it's hideous, but its worth a fortune. Kermit was charging a dollar for it. One dollar! And fifty cents apiece for the spoons.

A lot of people wanted to buy the spoons, but our neighbor was still there, and he kept saying my mother wouldn't want Kermit to sell them.

"You're darn right she wouldn't!" I said. "Kermit Albright, you're crazy! Mother would have a fit!"

"There's your mother now!" said the neighbor, and he pointed down the street.

My mother was walking fairly slowly, but just then a man went by in the other direction carrying Kermit's bedside lamp. My mother took one look at it and began to run.

That was the end of that. We had to close down our business right away, which was a pity because we had finally collected a crowd. But my mother grabbed the vase and the silver spoons and asked everybody to please go away. She wouldn't even let me sell the Nancy Drews, which were my own property.

As a matter of fact, my mother was really sore about the whole thing. I don't think I've ever seen her so mad in my whole life, either before or after. It wasn't just that we went outside when we promised we wouldn't. It was because she really cared about all that junk, hideous or not. She made us give her all the money, which came to over thirty dollars. Then I had to go around the neighborhood with her, trying to buy some of the stuff back. And I thought she would be grateful!

When we got back to the house, Kermit was all alone because Parker had left this little note for my mother saying thank you for the lovely time. She had gone home, even though she was supposed to stay for lunch. I was a little surprised, but when I mentioned it, my mother said she would have sent Parker home anyway. She was in such a bad mood that I suspected she must have sneaked into Swensen's for a couple of sundaes on her way back from the exhibit.

"Whatever made you do such a foolish thing?" my mother asked me.

I told her that I needed money really badly, so I

thought I'd earn a little while I waited for her to come home. "All things come to him who hustles while he waits," I told her. "Calvin Coolidge."

"I think that was Thomas Edison," said my mother, and she burst into tears. She and I did a lot of crying that fall!

The next day was Monday, and for once I woke up early, before the alarm. I lay in bed with my arms around Ronald, and gloomy thoughts kept running through my mind, even when I tried to push them out by deciding which cereal I'd have for breakfast.

First of all, my mother was still mad at me because the woman who bought the French omelette pan refused to sell it back. Second, my mother stopped my allowance until New Year's Day, so I was still forty-nine cents in the red. Third, the next day would be the first of December, and what had I accomplished? Exactly nothing. My plan was to track down Arabella and stage the big family reunion for Christmas Day. But if things didn't start moving, I wouldn't get that ad into *The Georgetowner* on time for the Christmas issue.

Thinking was so depressing that I decided to get up instead. For once I came downstairs before Kermit and finished the Sugar Corn Pops, which is the only cereal Kermit will eat, but even that didn't cheer me up. What was I going to do?

School wasn't as bad as usual that day. We had our eyes tested, and my class's turn came during math. Then when it was time for Spanish, instead of working, we got to make our costumes for the Christmas play. I made this fantastic paper mushroom that was purple with white spots on it, and I drew a big fat slug crawling on it, trailing slug juice. Señora Gonzalez didn't appreciate the slug, but she said it was too late to change it.

After lunch we had physical ed, which I usually detest. Every week I tell Mr. Butt I have an ulcer and I'm supposed to sit quietly and read a book, but Mr. Butt has a heart of stone.

This week when I reminded him about my ulcer, he just said, "That's interesting, Martha. Now, let's see a little more enthusiasm in your cartwheel."

If anybody can give me one good reason why a cartwheel is useful in life, I'll see what I can do about the enthusiasm. I mean, I'm not planning to be a cheerleader or advertise underpants on TV or anything. But Mr. Butt had us all doing cartwheels, and I was just thinking how lucky it was I never wear skirts when Wendy Hipp accidentally kicked Ali Zamara and Ali started to scream.

What happened was that Wendy wheeled down just when Ali was wheeling up, and Wendy was wearing clogs.

Well, Ali really kicked up a racket, and I could tell it was getting on Mr. Butt's nerves. First, he tried to kid Ali into admitting he was okay. Then he tried talking to him man to man with this tough but friendly voice. After that he tried some lovey-dovey stuff, but nothing worked. Ali kept on screaming.

Finally Mr. Butt got mad and told Ali to stop faking. Ali said he wasn't faking, so the school secretary called the rescue squad, and these paramedics put a splint on Ali's leg and carted him away in an ambulance.

It turned out that the only thing wrong with Ali was that his class was being tested in math that afternoon. A lot of the kids said mean things about him, but I felt kind of sympathetic. Besides, it sure livened up the day. What with one thing and another, I don't think we got around to school work at all until Tuesday!

As I said before, Tuesday was the first of December. I had made a resolution when I was lying in bed Monday morning that I would find a way to get that ad in the mail on the first of December if it killed me. And believe it or not, I did. On the second, not the first, but that was close enough.

On Tuesday I told all the kids in my class that if they lent me a nickel apiece, I would pay each of them back six cents. There were twenty-three of them, so the total came to $1.15. I have to admit math can come in handy if you're really in a pinch! During recess I asked a lot of other kids to lend me a nickel too, and most of them agreed.

Some of the kids didn't happen to have a nickel on them, but I got $1.45, and the others promised they would bring their nickels on Wednesday. So by Wednesday afternoon I had $4.04. I came up with four cents because some kid cheated me, but I didn't care. At least I was finally making progress! I had enough to get my ad in the mail, pay Kermit back, and buy some candy to celebrate.

*The Georgetowner* is a free newspaper. Sometimes they deliver it to your door, but mostly you just grab a copy while you're in some store or other. I got mine from the bank down the street. In fact, I took three because it was the first time I ever saw myself in print, and I thought I ought to save some copies to show my grandchildren.

My ad looked good. It was squeezed in between an ad for a massage in your own home and another about alterations in ladies' clothes. Stuck next to two boring things like that, it really hit your eye. "ARABELLA" was printed in big capital letters. I was really pleased!

One thing bothered me though. What if my mother saw it? She would recognize our phone number and want to know what I was up to. She had never been cooperative about helping me find my true parents, so I didn't want her involved until I had it all straightened out. And another problem was the Ables. If they saw my ad, for sure they would call up the number themselves. How would I explain?

I was worried for a while, but finally I had an idea. I went back to the bank and got two more copies of *The Georgetowner*. One of them I shoved through the Ables' mail slot and one through our own, so no one would have to pick up a copy in a store. But first I inked out my ad.

Naturally I expected to get a whole bunch of calls, so for the first few days I stayed close to the phone. But nothing happened. That is, about a thousand kids called up and wanted to talk to Kermit, but I kept telling them he wasn't there because I didn't want him to tie up the line. And a couple of people called for my mother. I finally had to let her talk to them because she got mad when she found out I had been saying she was out all week. But nobody called about Arabella.

Well, I began to get tired of sticking so close to the phone, and I could see Ronald didn't much like it either. One day I decided to run her up to the park for a change and take my chances on Arabella's calling while I was gone. I was just zipping up my jacket and looking around for Ronald's rope when the phone rang.

I ran to get there first, of course, and when I said hello, this squeaky foreign voice said, "Gooood ah-fter-nooon, theeees eeeez Ah-rrrabella!"

I was a little confused because it suddenly struck me that I hadn't planned what to say. But it turned out I didn't have to say anything because the squeaky voice started to giggle, and I knew straight off who it was. Parker!

I hung up. All I could think of was how I'd like to strangle Parker. I was furious and really embarrassed both at once. If we were still best friends, I might have warned her not to call, but as things were now, I couldn't trust her with my secret. One good thing: at least she got *me* on the phone and not my mother or Kermit!

Well, I was standing in Volta Park feeling kind of gloomy while Ronald sniffed all the trees to see if any of her friends had been around that day, when suddenly up walks Parker, grinning like an idiot.

"Very, very funny!" I told her.

Parker seemed to think it really was. "I recognized your phone number," she said after she got through laughing. "What's it all about? Who is Arabella?"

"It's a mistake," I told her. "They must have printed the wrong number or something. Now I suppose every nut in town will be calling us up."

Parker didn't believe me, but I refused to talk about it anymore.

In any case, that was the only call I ever got about Arabella, so all those weeks of worrying about my finances were for nothing. Now I had even bigger worries, and all because I had wasted $3.20. And for what? For the pleasure of hearing Parker play the idiot over the phone.

I now had a new problem. Eighty-one kids in school were after me to get back their six cents. Six, not five! When I promised I'd pay them interest, it didn't occur to me that eighty-one times one cent interest comes to eighty-one cents. Say eighty because I was darned if I'd pay interest to the kid who cheated me by one penny.

So now I owed $4.84, and believe me, some of those kids were getting nasty about it. My teacher said one day that I seemed to be making unhoped-for progress in math, and I told her: " 'Necessity is the mother of invention.' Calvin Coolidge."

Well, I may have been getting more popular with Ms. Folan, but the kids were about to lynch me. One morning I got to school, and two of them were marching around the playground with this big poster that said: "MARTHA ALBRIGHT IS A CROOK!"

Kermit grabbed it away and tore it up, which I must say was pretty brave of him, but all the same I decided I'd better do something about my debts, and fast!

To make things worse, I realized that Christmas was only a couple of weeks away, and there were all these people I wanted to buy presents for, but with what?

When we went to Saint Michael's that afternoon, I suggested playing bingo for money, but Larry said that was out, absolutely out. I told him it would save him the trouble of finding all those dumb play makeup kits, and it would probably cost less in the long run. Sondra said I should train my mind not to be so worldly. But I wasn't being worldly; I was just being practical. Besides, what could be more worldly than a play makeup kit?

Well, one Saturday I was paying a visit to the Ables, and they asked me to stay for lunch. At first I said no thanks because there was this really disgusting smell in the house that Amory Able said was kippered herring. But Maud must have guessed what I was thinking because she said she would make me a ham sandwich, so I stayed.

The three of us sat around the kitchen table, kind of chatting. That is, Maud and I chatted while Amory picked apart his kippered herring. It looked just like something the cats pull out of the garbage and spread around the back alley. When I mentioned it, Amory Able said that Calvin Coolidge ate kippered herring every day of his life for breakfast, which I don't believe for one minute—not unless they built him a smell-proof room at the White House.

Anyway, we got to talking about Christmas, and I told the Ables how worried I was that I couldn't buy presents for the people on my list. From the way Maud listened, I could tell she really understood how I was feeling. Not Amory, though. He spat out a bone and said, "Poppycock!"

"We were talking about Christmas, dear!" said Maud reproachfully.

"That's right," said Amory Able. "Poppycock! Christmas is just one more damn fool excuse for moral and gastronomic dissipation."

I wasn't quite sure what he meant, so I thought it was safer to agree with him, but Maud started bleating things about Baby Jesus and the angels.

"It sounds very pretty to talk about angels," said

Amory Able, "but what it comes right down to is commerce! Christmas was invented by shopkeepers. Now when I was a boy, I never expected a lot of fancy store-bought presents. I used to play for days on end with a stick and a piece of string."

"What did you do with them?" I asked. I was interested to know because maybe I could give Kermit a stick and a piece of string for Christmas and it wouldn't cost me a cent.

But either Amory Able couldn't remember back that far or it was something he didn't think he should tell me because instead of answering, he stuffed in a big mouthful of kippered herring, bones and all, and started to chew.

Maud was still thinking about my problem. "Why don't you give homemade presents, dear?" she asked me. "Homemade presents are the nicest because they show how much you care."

I remembered all those ashtrays that Kermit and I had made in school. Some of them dated back to kindergarten—the kind where you just press your hand into the clay and the teacher bakes and glazes it for you. I always thought they looked pretty silly, but my mother puts them out for guests all the same. Why not make Christmas presents out of clay? I consider myself fairly artistic, so I was sure I could come up with some good ideas.

Of course there was the same old problem: clay costs money. But we have this handicraft book for kids, and I found a recipe for clay that you can make yourself. It looked really easy. All you do is mix hot water and salt and flour. So on Sunday afternoon when my mother was out with Kermit, I went into the kitchen and started to mix. The whole time I was mixing I planned my Christmas list.

We definitely didn't need any more ashtrays because my mother bought back most of the crystal ones that I had gotten rid of at the tag sale. Besides, she doesn't smoke. But I thought I might make her a bowl to put pins and things in, and maybe another for Maud Able. Kermit would like a locomotive, and it would be fun to make a dish shaped like a fish for Amory Able to eat kippered herring out of.

I went on imagining all the presents I was going to make, and then suddenly I stared into the mixing bowl. It didn't look like enough for more than one or two things, but already I had used up all the flour and salt in the house. I didn't think adding more hot water would help.

I looked in the cupboards and found some stuff I thought might make good clay: confectioner's sugar and oatmeal and baking soda and cornmeal and garlic salt and mashed-potato mix. I dumped it all in, and it seemed to work just fine. So I made my presents, and they looked pretty good, except maybe for the locomotive, which was a little lopsided. I put them in the oven on cookie sheets and set the heat at three hundred the way the book said. Then I took Ronald for a walk.

Well, when we came back, my mother and Kermit were already home, and I was in trouble again. For someone with good intentions, I sure get in a lot of trouble. Mostly it's never my fault, so I must be unlucky.

There was this terrible smell, which I think maybe was the garlic. I had been a little doubtful about adding garlic salt, but I thought once the clay was baked, the smell would go away. Instead, it got worse. There was a lot of smoke in the kitchen, and my mother had all the windows open and the fan on. She didn't look too pleased.

"You didn't open the oven, did you?" I asked her. "It was supposed to be a surprise!"

"It *was* a surprise," said my mother. "And I have a surprise for *you*. As soon as the oven cools off, you're going to clean it."

I opened the oven door and looked in. Guess what? I must have added something wrong because the clay rose, and the things didn't keep their same shape when they got bigger. Instead, they got all glopped together and ran off the cookie sheets. It was disgusting.

You would have thought cleaning that oven was punishment enough, but when my mother saw how much stuff was missing from the cupboards, she was even madder and said I had to replace it out of my allowance.

I had been making this big effort not to cry about things so easily, and I had done pretty well since the tag sale, but this was too much. I stood there bawling like a baby, and my tears sizzled when they dropped on the open door. If I hadn't felt so awful, it would have been funny.

My mother groaned and sat down on a kitchen stool. "Martha, sweetie, what's going on?" she asked. "You were beginning to look positively happy a while back, and now everything seems to be going wrong again. What's the problem?"

"You'd cry too if you owed six cents to practically every kid in school," I told her.

Naturally my mother wanted to know how I got so deeply in debt, but I couldn't stop crying to explain, so she dropped the subject. Instead, she started talking about where the three of us should go when she got her vacation. We had been discussing it for weeks. My mother wanted to go to the mountains and ski, but Kermit and I were working on her to take us to Disneyworld. So far we hadn't made much progress.

By the time I got through explaining that you could swim at Disneyworld and that swimming was healthier than skiing, I felt a whole lot better. My mother still didn't say yes about Disneyworld, but she was really nice about my debts. She said I didn't have to pay for the groceries after all, and when we got back from our vacation, wherever it was, she would find me some jobs to do.

After vacation? Big help! I might be dead by then. Meanwhile, I had no money, no presents, no friends at school, and exactly twelve more days until Christmas!

# Chapter
## 9

The following week was what you might call the low point of my career. I had practically given up finding Arabella before Christmas. My only hope would be advertising in the *Washington Post* or even *The New York Times*, but there's no way to pay for daily ads when you're bankrupt. As it was, I expected the local police to turn up at the door and drag me off to jail for cheating eighty kids out of six cents apiece.

No one was speaking to me at school. That is, the kids were speaking *at* me, threatening to get their moms to call my mom and all that, but otherwise they wouldn't have anything to do with me.

The worst was during physical ed, when both captains refused to choose me for their teams when I was the last one left. Mr. Butt had to let me help him referee.

I would sit all day at my desk thinking how Arabella and my dog-trainer father would feel sorry for me if they knew what I was going through. I was pinning great hopes on my dog-trainer father. If he had been there to advise me, I never would have gotten into this mess. In fact, even my adoptive father might be a help if he were at home.

Then I got to thinking about my adoptive father off in South America, and suddenly I started missing him so much that it hurt. I mean all at once, without any warning, as if I had been storing it all up inside me since September. So right there in school I wrote this letter to my adoptive father telling him how everything was going wrong and could he please, please come home soon. For Christmas, if possible.

I didn't mention the fact that Ronald was still living with us. By Christmas I hoped to have persuaded Amory Able to take her, if necessary.

I was supposed to be working on my science report, and I guess Ms. Folan could tell I wasn't because she crept up behind me and grabbed the letter, saying, "What's this, Martha?"

At first I thought she was going to get mad, but after she read the letter, she just handed it back and told me to hurry up with my project because it was almost time for lunch.

When the others went down to the cafeteria, Ms. Folan asked me to stay behind a minute. She said all these sloppy things about my father serving his country by working for the government in South America, and I should be proud of him, which I guess I was. I began to feel a little better, but then she said not to get my hopes up about Christmas because it took a long time for letters to get to that part of South America.

I gave the letter to my mother, and she mailed it along with a couple of drawings Kermit did. "Have you two wrapped your Christmas presents for Daddy?" she asked.

I felt terrible. "I'm going to make something, but it isn't ready yet," I mumbled. I could see she thought I had forgotten.

"Mine is ready," said Kermit. "I finished all my Christmas presents in November."

I followed Kermit up to his room and asked what he was giving everyone for Christmas. I was hoping he could give me a useful idea or two.

"I can't show you yours," said Kermit, "because I want it to be a surprise. But I'll show you all the others."

He got this big box out of his cupboard, and when I looked inside, I nearly threw up. He had taken some paper plates and pasted paper doilies on them. Then on each doily he had written someone's name—with dead caterpillars.

"Yuck!" I said. "How did you do it?"

"It was my own idea," he told me proudly. "I used glue for the caterpillars, and then I glazed it with hair spray. Don't touch. It's fragile!"

I wasn't about to touch. All I could think of was how there must be this paper plate somewhere with "Martha" written on it in dead caterpillars, and when I opened Kermit's present on Christmas morning, I'd have to look really surprised and happy. I told him it was a great idea, but it didn't give me much help for making presents of my own.

Everybody was all excited about Christmas at Saint Michael's. Larry had been thumping and bumping Christmas carols on his guitar for weeks, and Sondra stopped dancing with her bottom stuck out and started gliding around looking soulful, as if she were praying. We were going to have this big party after the last day of school, with a super-duper jackpot in bingo and prizes for everyone. Meanwhile, we were supposed to make Christmas cards for all our friends.

I sat there wondering who to make cards for when suddenly I got this idea that I hoped would help me out with my debts at school. I made eighty Christmas cards out of construction paper, and on each one I wrote: "Merry Christmas, Wendy!" or Ali, or Carlos, or whatever. "Remember Baby Jesus, and if you promise to wait until January, I'll make it seven cents."

The other kids began to complain that I was using up all the paper, so Sondra came over to see, and she got mad. Not just about the paper, I mean, but about what she called my materialism, which means you think that only money counts. I looked it up. She dumped my cards in the trash, which I guess was just as well because come to think of it, in January I would have been deeper in debt than ever.

I asked Amory Able what were his ideas about materialism when I paid him a visit the next Saturday. He brought up the same old story about his stick and a piece of string. This time I got him to tell me what he did with them. There are thirty-seven things you can do with a stick and a piece of string, but you would have to be bored to tears to try any of them.

All the same, I asked Maud Able for a piece of string, and I got a stick from their backyard and wrapped them both up to make a Christmas present for Kermit. I enclosed Amory Able's list too, in case Kermit needed instructions. It wasn't the most exciting present in the world, but I figured it rated with a bunch of dead cater-pillars.

Maud Able told me how glad she was I had decided on homemade presents. "What are you making for your mother, dear?" she asked.

"Nothing," I said, and I described my failure with the clay.

When Maud heard about the ashtrays Kermit and I had made my parents over the years, even though they didn't smoke, she laughed.

"When I was a girl," she said, "I made my mother two pincushions a year, Christmas and birthday. My mother hated to sew, so she never used them, but she kept them lined up on her knickknack shelf until she died."

"My mother doesn't even have *one* pincushion," I told her. "Are they hard to make?"

Before I knew it, Maud had her sewing basket out and she was pulling out scraps of silk and cuttings of old lace.

Now, I'm no hand with a needle, but I decided I would make that pincushion if it killed me. And it nearly did. The trouble was that Maud made me wear this little silver gadget called a thimble. It kept getting in the way, so I had to keep that finger in the air. The other fingers weren't too good at pushing the needle in and out. After my right hand got all bloody, I switched to my left.

Amory Able sat beside me the whole time I was sewing. I was concentrating too hard to talk, but that didn't bother him. First he recited "The Ballad of One-Eye Mike." Then he told me the best way to prepare kippered herring, what to do for frostbite, and how to lean your hoe against the wall so no one steps on the blade part and gets conked on the head by the stick part.

He also told me the only proper way to address an envelope and explained how high a million dollars would be if you piled a million one-dollar bills on top of each other. The answer is: higher than the Washington Monument. Then, in case I forgot, he told me how much it cost to buy a loaf of bread back when he was a boy. I guess he didn't have much to do that afternoon.

I was trying to write my mother's initials in cross-stitch—in no way an easy job. It was lucky Maud wouldn't let me keep the pins between my lips because suddenly Amory Able shouted so loud that I would have swallowed my pins.

"What's the matter?" I asked.

"Look at that 'O'!" he yelled. "You're sewing it counterclockwise!"

"It's easier that way," I told him. "That's the way I always do it."

Amory Able stood up and puffed his chest out. "There are only two ways of doing things!" he said. "My way and the wrong way."

"Calvin Coolidge?" I asked.

"Who else?" he snapped, and he stomped out of the room.

When I finished the pincushion, I showed it to Maud. For a moment I thought she was going to laugh. Then she said, "Very nice, dear! And I know an excellent recipe for removing blood stains."

I thought the blood stains added a personal touch, but Maud removed them all the same. Then she wrapped the pincushion and sent me home. I was late for supper.

That pincushion had taken me four and a half hours to sew!

I felt pretty good when I went to bed, but the next morning was a different matter.

Some people wake up feeling terrific, but I'm just the opposite. Before I even open my eyes, I think of whatever trouble I'm in, which is usually a lot. This morning was Sunday, so I had plenty of time to think. It was as if someone were holding a piece of paper an inch away from my nose with this list on it:

1. What are you going to give for Christmas?
2. How are you going to pay the kids at school?
3. When are you going to get up the nerve to ask the Ables to keep Ronald Reagan?
4. You forgot to vacuum all week, so today you have to do the whole house.

My conscience kept nagging me about the vacuuming, so I got out of bed and set to work. I started with the stairs, which looked like the monkey cage at the zoo because Kermit and I had been eating peanuts there. But before I finished the first step, my mother slammed her door open so hard that the knob made a hole in the wall outside her room.

I told you that my mother hardly ever raises her voice. That probably accounts for why when she does, it's ten times louder than anyone else's. It drowned out the noise of our vacuum, which I didn't think was possible.

"Do you want to wake up the whole neighborhood?" she yelled. "It's only six o'clock, damn it! I work like a slave all week, and on Sunday my kids have to wake me up at six!" Then she slammed her door closed again.

Well, I turned off the vacuum and went to look at the clock. She was right: two minutes past six. Now what was I going to do? Somehow I didn't feel like going back to bed.

I went down to the kitchen, and by the time I had finished the Sugar Corn Pops, it began to get lighter outside. It looked like a nice day, even though the thermometer said only nineteen. I bundled up and took Ronald out for a walk.

While Ronald was sniffing at the lampposts making up her mind, which takes forever, I thought how unfair it is that whenever I do something really helpful, someone gets mad at me.

It had been drizzling the day before, and all the puddles had frozen into splintery sheets of ice. If you stomp on them, it makes a fantastic noise. I stomped all the puddles on my block, but the ones on the next block were already stomped. I looked around to see who else could be stomping puddles so early in the morning, and there was Parker, sitting on her front steps.

"Hi there, pickle-face!" she said.

I probably did look sour. I certainly *felt* sour. "Good morning, Bettysue," I said.

Parker made a face. "Martha, could you please, *please*, call me Parker again?" she asked.

I wasn't too sure about that, so I changed the subject. "What are you doing out here so early?" I asked her.

Parker told me that she woke up at six by mistake,

and her mother got mad at her for practicing her French out loud. Parker's school has French instead of Spanish.

"That's funny!" I said. "The same thing happened to me." And I told her about the vacuum.

"It's unfair, isn't it!" said Parker. "Just when you do something virtuous for once, someone gets mad at you."

We got to talking, and Parker was being friendly like in the old days, so before I knew it, I told her all the things that had been bothering me since school started. That is, I told her about my money problems and how worried I was about Ronald Reagan, but I didn't tell her about Arabella because I wasn't sure I could trust her with my secret.

Parker was really understanding. She kept nodding and saying, "Oh, I know how you feel!"

When I reached the part about the clay that rose, she got all excited. "I have lots of clay!" she said. "My aunt gave me a whole barrelful for my birthday. Let's go and make some stuff!"

So we went inside, and I made all those things over again: the fish plate and the bowls and the locomotive and a penholder for my father, in case he got a new White House pen. We baked them, and they turned out fine. It was a big relief because when I told Parker about the stick and the piece of string, she was really shocked.

"If you gave that to me for Christmas, I'd put worms in your bed!" she told me. Parker really likes Kermit.

At least now I was giving Kermit a real present, and this time the locomotive didn't come out lopsided. Parker thought it was supposed to be a dinosaur, but when I explained, she said, come to think of it, it looked more like a locomotive.

Well, I stayed all morning at Parker's, and then she came to my house and we made fudge. My mother walked into the kitchen right in the middle of it. She probably smelled chocolate and just couldn't keep away. She kept fussing around and fidgeting and looking over our shoulders. It made me nervous.

"The fudge won't be ready for ages!" I told her. "It hasn't even reached the soft-ball stage yet. Don't worry. We'll save you some."

My mother looked embarrassed. "I think what I really had on my mind is that I owe you an apology. I'm sorry I yelled at you this morning, Martha. It's just that six o'clock is a little early for vacuuming."

" 'Beggars can't be choosers'!" I told her. "Calvin Coolidge."

"John Heywood," said my mother. "We're not exactly beggars. I think maybe we should get a new vacuum cleaner after all. I found one in a catalogue that's supposed to be whisper soft."

"Don't believe everything you read," I advised her. "If you've got money to throw away, how about lending me some? I'll pay interest!"

"Your mom is nice!" said Parker when my mother finally left the kitchen. "You're lucky you didn't get stuck with parents who believe in private schools."

"Hey, wait a minute!" I said, and I stared at her.

Parker turned beet red and started buttering the pan, even though she knew perfectly well that it was already buttered. I was about to say something else, but then I shut my mouth. Parker was my friend again, and that was all that mattered.

The next morning I didn't feel quite so terrible

when I woke up, but one thing was sure: I didn't dare go to school! The kids had been so nasty about getting their money back that on Friday I absolutely swore they would get six cents apiece on Monday. Now it was Monday.

Some of the kids in my class had written a petition that they were taking around to all the other kids to sign. They said if I didn't pay my debts, they were going to send it to the President. I know that the President has enough to worry about, but I wouldn't put it past him to send the petition to the mayor. My father says this is called relegation in politics, and it happens all the time.

I tried to think whether I had anything to sell fast, for instant cash. Suddenly at breakfast it occurred to me that I *did* own something that was worth enough money to pay my debts and get my ad into the dailies as well. That was my gold chain.

As soon as we got out the front door that morning, I told Kermit I was going to be late to school.

"You'll be in trouble!" he warned me.

"I'll be in trouble whatever I do," I told him, "but if this works out, the trouble won't be quite so bad."

Anyway, I took my chain down to the jewelry store on Wisconsin Avenue, and I had to wait a whole hour until it opened. It was a complete waste of time because the man behind the counter said how beautiful my chain was and everything, but he wouldn't give me any money for it. Instead, he wrote out this receipt to say he was keeping it for evaluation.

I asked the man what evaluation meant. He said it meant he had to find out how much the chain was worth, but as long as I had the receipt, he couldn't steal it from me. I kept telling him how hard up I was. I even said I'd settle for five dollars down and the rest later, but all he did was ask for my name and telephone number to put down on the receipt, so I gave up and left.

You can imagine how I felt on my way back to school. Not only was I going to have my teacher on my back and maybe even get sent to the principal's office again, but the kids were going to kill me. I just knew they would.

Well, the funny thing is, when I walked into the classroom, the teacher smiled and said, "Good morning, Martha! Is everything all right now?"

The kids all said, "Hi, Martha!" in this really friendly way.

That was fine with me, so I sat down and got to work, but as soon as the bell rang for recess, I found Kermit and asked him what was going on.

"I told Ms. Folan that you had this really huge splinter and you had to go to the emergency ward to have it taken out," he said.

If Kermit weren't my brother, I would have kissed him, right there in the middle of the playground. "But what came over all the kids?" I asked him. "Why are they being so nice all of a sudden?"

"Oh, that!" said Kermit. "Parker was over here before school started, and she paid them off."

I was in a daze. I couldn't eat my lunch, and I was so absentminded during math that for once I gave the right answer. Even at Saint Michael's that afternoon, Larry came over and said how really cooperative I was being.

"Are you feeling sick?" he asked. "Or are you hopefully turning over a new leaf?"

I was too dazed to tell him where to get off.

All I could think of was what a terrific friend Parker was and I wondered how I could pay her back. Not with money, I mean—she would get that anyway—but with something that would show how really grateful I was. It made me feel terrible that I didn't have a present for her, not even out of clay.

It wasn't until we were eating supper that I suddenly remembered my chain. I didn't need to sell it now, but maybe it was too late. That jeweler had probably sold it to somebody else named Martha or had melted it down for the precious eighteen-karat gold.

"Are the stores closed yet?" I asked my mother.

"Yes," she said firmly, "and even if they weren't, it's too late to go out."

I thought maybe I could telephone, so I went to look up the number of the store, but just then the phone rang. My mother answered, and you guessed it—it was the jeweler. He's a lily-livered, double-crossing rat, and when I grow up and get rich, I'll never get any of my jewelry from him, not even if it's free.

But that's not the point. The point is that when my mother got off the phone, she had this really scary expression on her face. I thought it was a good time to vacuum Kermit's room, but she grabbed my wrist and looked me straight in the eye.

"All right, Martha," she said. "What's this all about?"

# Chapter 10

I can be very stubborn when I like. As far as I was concerned, my mother could pull out my fingernails with red-hot iron pincers. I still wasn't about to tell her one single thing I didn't feel like telling her.

She kept saying, "But *why*, Martha?"

All I would answer was, "I told you I was in debt. Didn't you believe me?"

But my mother is smarter than she looks. She kept on asking these tricky, unfair questions until she wormed it all out of me.

"You seriously think that Amory Able is your grandfather?" my mother asked in a choked-up voice.

I thought she was going to cry. I mean, she had always been sensitive about this adoption business. But instead, she burst out laughing. I was a little offended.

"What about my unsociable disposition?" I demanded. "What about all those baby pictures that accidentally-on-purpose got lost in Brussels? And what about my green eyes?"

My mother stopped laughing and put her arms around me. "Are you really serious, sweetie?" she asked. "I was telling the truth about the baby pictures. Ours were lost, but your grandparents have a few copies they could show you. And you got your green eyes from my own mother. Didn't you ever notice Grandma's eyes? Why, you look just like her!"

"I thought two people with brown eyes *couldn't* have a child with green eyes!" I protested. "I thought it just wasn't possible!"

"Well, it is," said my mother. "I don't know what put that idea in your head. Now, come with me and we'll get this straight once and for all."

She took me to her room, and I watched while she rummaged in her files and came up with this piece of paper. She was about to show it to me, but suddenly she grinned and held it behind her back.

"Before you see this, I want you to know one thing," said my mother. "We didn't choose you—nature chose you for us. But if we *did* have to choose, you're exactly what we'd want. Disposition included."

Very funny! I held my hand out for the paper, which was my birth certificate. It said when I was born and who my parents were, and they weren't Arabella and a dog trainer. They were the parents I had been living with all along, which I guess is more convenient, if you come right down to it. Except that a dog trainer might have given me some good advice on what to do with Ronald.

Well, that kind of dampened my spirits for a while, but I couldn't stay depressed for long because of the excitement of Christmas. Even school was fun for a change, and the best thing of all was that Parker's mother called up my mother and asked if Kermit and I could come to their house that week instead of going to Saint Michael's.

"Well, I don't know if they'll want to," my mother told her. "There's some sort of Christmas party coming up."

Kermit and I were standing by the phone. My mother put her hand over the receiver and asked us, "You wouldn't want to miss the Saint Michael's Christmas party, would you?"

We both screamed, "YES!"

My mother was surprised, but she wasn't nearly as surprised as I was. I thought Kermit was crazy about Saint Michael's!

"I wouldn't go to the Saint Michael's Christmas party even if I won the super-duper jackpot, and for once it was a book!" I told my mother.

And Kermit added, "A person can get awfully tired of playing bingo."

My mother looked as if she were having second thoughts about Saint Michael's. It was about time!

In the evenings we were really busy at home, but I thought my mother looked a little sad. It was the first time we ever had Christmas without my father, and that raised another problem. I knew that Christmas morning would go all right, but what about the afternoon? Other years just when we were getting that let-down, over-stuffed feeling, my father would pile us all in the car and drive us to the zoo. No matter what city we were living in, he always found a zoo.

You probably think we're crazy going to the zoo on

Christmas, but my father said the animals needed cheering up. So we would sing carols outside all their cages, and other people usually joined in too. I couldn't imagine going to the zoo without my father, but staying home might be even worse.

"Are we going to the zoo this year?" I asked my mother on Wednesday evening while we were making Christmas cookies.

She had obviously been thinking about the problem herself because she answered right away. "Maybe we should do something different for a change."

"Like what?" asked Kermit.

He was making his own tray of cookies. He had mixed all this food coloring together until it was a kind of muddy purple, and he was rolling the dough into little purple worms. It was disgusting. I don't know why my mother lets him do that sort of thing, and besides, his hands were filthy.

"If the Food and Drug Administration came in and saw you doing that, they'd put you in jail," I told Kermit.

"It's for Daddy," said Kermit. "I'm going to put them in a cookie tin and send them to South America."

I was sure my mother would put a damper on that plan right away, but she didn't say a word. She spoils Kermit terribly, and if he got put in jail, she'd probably just bail him out.

"It'll get seized at the customs, and then you'll really be in trouble," I said. "It's germ warfare. You'll create an international incident."

My mother took Kermit's cookie tray and popped it into the oven. "Nonsense, Martha!" she said. "Where's your Christmas spirit? I think we're all forgetting the true meaning of Christmas. My idea for this year is the same as at Thanksgiving. We're going to share with someone old and lonely."

My mother is a real masochist. She's unhappy enough without my father around, so what does she do? She invites someone she doesn't even like, to make it worse. This time she had two people in mind. You guessed it: Mrs. McGrath and Mr. Purse.

Luckily she never got around to inviting them, though, because just then the doorbell rang. It was Maud and Amory Able. My mother asked them in for a drink and some cookies, but Amory Able said no thank you, they had just stepped outside for a constitutional.

I've heard of unconstitutional, but constitutional was new to me. My mother says it's like jogging, but I suspect she's wrong. Somehow I can't see Maud Able jogging.

Anyway, Maud explained that they had stopped by to deliver an invitation. "We would like to return your hospitality," she said. "We hoped you would join us for Christmas dinner, after church."

My mother had this funny look on her face, which I guessed was because it hadn't occurred to her to go to church. I helped her out by changing the subject.

"Who is going to cook?" I asked.

People are never grateful! My mother looked at me as if I had said something really bad. "Martha!" she said in this sort of threatening growl.

"I didn't mean to be rude," I explained. "I was just wondering whether Mr. Able is planning to serve us banana-salami stew."

Maud's eyes twinkled. I think she really understands me. "I'll be cooking, dear," she said, "and I hope you all can come. Christmas is such a sacred time. Don't you agree?"

I tried to think of something religious to say back, but I didn't get a chance.

"Poppycock!" said Amory Able. He thumped his cane on the front steps and scowled. "Christmas is nothing but one more damn fool excuse to—"

Before he could say anything worse, Maud grabbed his elbow and pulled him away. I never saw her move so fast!

"Don't worry," I told my mother when they had gone. "We don't have to accept if you don't want to."

But my mother said it wasn't such a bad idea. I suppose she was still thinking about my father and the zoo.

Christmas morning is usually a mixed bag, meaning that Kermit and I tend to wake up at about five-thirty, and my parents tend to sleep longer than any other morning of the year. The rule is that we open our stockings on their bed, but what usually happens is that my father says something rude, and my mother says, "Please don't swear, darling. It's Christmas!"

Then Kermit and I have to go back to bed, which is torture.

This Christmas my father wasn't there, and Kermit and I had an idea. When we woke up at five-thirty, Kermit snuck into my mother's room and set her clock ahead two hours while I ran downstairs to unhook the stockings from the mantelpiece.

My mother wasn't too happy, but when she saw that

it was seven-thirty, she let us stay. "Why is it so dark?" she grumbled. "I hope it doesn't rain!"

My mother graduated top of her class from college, but her mind doesn't start to function until after breakfast. Anyway, we opened our stockings, and then we told her she could go back to sleep.

"That's the best present you could give me!" my mother said, and she pulled the pillow over her head.

She never noticed Kermit setting the clock back to the right time, which was twenty to six.

In our family we don't get important things in our stockings because the real presents come later, after breakfast. Instead, we get a lot of candy and maybe a joke or two. Kermit and I sat on my bed eating candy and waiting for my mother to wake up again. An hour went by, and then another hour. There wasn't a sound from her room.

"Do you think she's dead?" Kermit asked as he stuffed another Hershey bar into his mouth.

"I wouldn't dare go find out before eight o'clock," I told him.

So we kept on eating our Christmas candy until there was nothing left in either stocking and I was beginning to feel peculiar. I had an idea that if I stood up, I might feel a little better, and when I did, this one last Hershey bar fell off the bed.

"That's mine!" said Kermit, and he made a lunge for it.

I don't know why I didn't just let him have it. I really didn't feel too good, even standing up. Besides, the Hershey bar was all warm and mushy. I must have been sitting on it. But they say indigestion gives you a bad temper. I snatched it back.

"You stole it and you were hiding it from me!" said Kermit. "You're a pig and you have a stomach like a blimp!"

I don't happen to appreciate remarks about my figure, which isn't as bad as all that, and anyway, I'd rather be plump than skinny like Kermit. It made me mad, so I grabbed Kermit by the shoulders and started shaking him and yelling at him, and I accidentally kicked the switch on his train set that makes all the locomotives whistle at once.

Eight locomotives can make a lot of noise. My mother burst into the room shouting, "What in the name of—!"

Whose name it was I never found out because Kermit threw up—on me!

My mother said, "I am so fed up with you two that I—" and she ran for a towel.

"If your father were here he would—" she went on, and she started wiping up the mess.

"Martha, don't stand there like an idiot! Go put those filthy slippers in the—"

"I wish you'd finish your sentences," I told her.

My mother threw the towel down and started yelling at me, with her mouth about two inches from my face. For someone who rarely raises her voice, she certainly did a lot of yelling that year.

"I'll finish *this* sentence!" my mother said. "You two are cleaning up this mess! I'm going back to bed, and I plan to stay there. And if I hear one squeak out of you, I'm going to call the Salvation Army and tell them to cart the whole business away, tree and all. I don't know who invented Christmas, but I'll bet you he didn't have kids!"

She ran out of breath, which gave me time to tell her that Christmas was invented by shopkeepers. "Christmas is just one more damn fool excuse for moral and gastronomic dissipation," I told her. "Calvin Coolidge."

My mother slammed the door. There had been a lot of door-slamming that morning, and I began to be afraid the neighbors would complain.

"We'd better be quiet," I told Kermit.

Kermit agreed. He was awfully pale, and I felt a little guilty. "You can have that Hershey bar," I said. "I don't care."

When I mentioned the Hershey bar, Kermit looked even worse, so I changed the subject quickly. "It's unlucky to fight on a holy day," I told him. "Maybe we ought to say a prayer, just to be safe."

Kermit said he couldn't remember any prayers. All he could remember was his times tables and the flag salute. So we said the flag salute because I wasn't about to spoil Christmas with the sevens tables, which I hadn't bothered to write on my fingers anyway since school let out.

You probably won't believe this, but my mother didn't come out of her room until eleven-thirty that morning, and when she did, she looked terrible.

Kermit and I didn't dare say a word all during breakfast, and we kept on looking at the clock. The second Christmas rule in our family is that you don't get to open the important presents until after a healthy breakfast, but it was already close to noon. We were due at the Ables at one o'clock.

I told my mother politely that Kermit and I were full of candy, and eggs were known to be bad for upset stomachs.

"We'll get cholesterol," I said. "When they open us up, we'll have fat around our hearts."

My mother didn't say anything. She doesn't like to talk until she's had about a gallon of coffee.

"We're supposed to eat lunch in an hour," I reminded her. "The Ables will think it's rude if we don't have any appetites."

My mother put two slices of bacon on my plate. Usually I'm crazy about bacon because it's such a treat; my mother doesn't have time to cook it on weekdays. But this morning I couldn't stand the sight of it.

"We won't have time to open our presents!" I said.

"And whose fault will that be?" my mother snapped.

She poured herself another cup of coffee and shut her eyes, the way she does when she has a headache. Who else's mother would have a headache on Christmas morning? There was no arguing with her. She took her time over breakfast, and then she cleaned everything up, even the bacon pan.

When my mother finally finished, she sent Kermit and me to our rooms to get all dolled up. I had to wear my party dress, which I detest, and Kermit had to slick his hair down and put on this dumb gray-flannel suit with white knee socks and short pants. We both looked stupid.

My mother was waiting downstairs dressed in something fancy. She was wearing lipstick, too. "Are you ready to go?" she asked. "Where is Ronald's leash?"

I'm always losing Ronald's leash because I use it only when my mother comes too. While I was hunting for it, Kermit went into the living room and looked at the tree.

"We never opened any presents!" he wailed, as if it were the first time he noticed. "We can't go out and leave all our presents there!"

"We can and we will!" said my mother. "Next Christmas maybe you'll remember and try to behave yourselves—if it's humanly possible."

She certainly was in a bad mood. I couldn't understand it. I was for giving in, since we didn't have time anyway, but Kermit turned pale again. I could see my mother was afraid for his gray flannel suit.

"All right, Kermit," she said with a sigh. "You can open a small one. But hurry!"

"I don't want to open mine yet," said Kermit. "I want you to open yours!"

He had this really sweet, anxious expression on his face. My mother relaxed a little and smiled. "I'm sorry," she said. "Run and get your present for me, and I'll open it now. The Ables won't mind if we're a few minutes late."

Well, Kermit ran and got my mother's present. It was all done up in tissue paper that he had painted himself with water colors, and my mother made a big fuss about unwrapping it.

"What can it be?" she kept asking. "It's too light for a book, and it's the wrong shape for an ashtray, and it doesn't rattle like candy."

"Don't rattle it!" Kermit warned her.

But my mother didn't listen. She was concentrating on getting the paper off without tearing it. Then she shut her eyes.

"Don't tell me what it is!" she said. "I'm going to guess."

My mother put her hand inside the package and let out a scream so loud that I'm surprised the neighbors didn't call the police.

"What's the matter?" I asked.

My mother brought out a fistful of dead caterpillars and screamed again. I guess when she shook the package, they all fell off the plate. I burst out laughing, which wasn't very nice because Kermit started to cry, but I couldn't help it. To make things worse, Ronald thought some invisible stranger was attacking her family. She tore around in circles snapping at the air and barking her head off.

Just then the front door opened, and this angry voice shouted, "WHAT ON EARTH IS GOING ON?"

It was my father.

You should have heard the silence. I stopped laughing, Kermit stopped crying, my mother stopped screaming, and Ronald Reagan went scooting upstairs and hid under my bed.

My father stepped into the house and shut the door behind him.

"Correct me if I'm wrong," he said, "but isn't this Christmas?"

# Chapter
## 11

It took us a while to get things straightened out. My mother was clutching my father so hard around the neck that I thought she'd strangle him. After my father got her to let go, he had to cheer Kermit up by admiring his plates. He even found the glue and helped Kermit write my mother's name with caterpillars again. I don't know how he did it. I mean, I told Kermit what a great idea it was, but I wouldn't touch those dead caterpillars for anything in the world.

"Why couldn't you just buy your mother a box of candy like normal kids?" I asked Kermit.

Kermit answered, " 'A fool and his money are soon parted.' Calvin Coolidge!"

"I have had Calvin Coolidge up to *here!*" my mother moaned. "If I get any more of him at lunch today, I'm going to scream!"

"You've screamed enough this morning," I told her. "I'll try to steer him onto Robert Service instead."

"I can't stand Robert Service!" said Kermit. "If I hear any more Robert Service, I'll throw up."

"Poppycock!" I shouted.

My father stared at us as if we three had all gone out of our minds. "I've been away too long," he said. "What's this all about?"

"You'll see," I promised him.

My mother wanted to call up the Ables and say that we couldn't go after all, but when she explained to my father, he said it wasn't fair.

"They've probably been preparing for days, and they'll be hurt if you don't turn up," he said. "Besides, I'm looking forward to my Christmas turkey."

"You'll be lucky if it's turkey," I warned him. "If Amory Able helped with the cooking, we'll end up in the emergency ward at Georgetown Hospital."

My father ran upstairs to change out of his traveling clothes, and while he was gone, I had a few minutes to think.

Half of me was so happy he was back that I could have cried. The other half knew it meant the end of Ronald Reagan, and that made me want to cry too. What was I going to do?

I went over to the window and looked out. It had snowed the night before, making it a white Christmas. Every year Kermit and I pray for a white Christmas, but this year it just made things worse. Would I have to turn Ronald out into the snow? It looked awfully cold.

Suddenly I had an idea. So far I hadn't had the nerve to ask the Ables to take in Ronald, but what if I just plain gave Ronald to them for Christmas? Even if they weren't too pleased, it wouldn't be polite to refuse.

So I ran and got a huge piece of red ribbon and tied it around Ronald's neck with a big bow. Then I made a little card that said "Season's Greetings, Love from Martha!" and pinned it to the ribbon. The whole time I was doing it, Ronald licked my face. I couldn't decide whether it was because she was sorry for me or whether it was just because she liked the taste of tears.

When my father came downstairs again, he took one look at the red ribbon and groaned. "I don't want to spoil the day by asking why that mutt is still with us," he told me, "but don't you think it would be wiser to leave her here?"

I refused. "You can't lock up your dog on Christmas Day," I said. "It's unconstitutional. Besides, Ronald is crazy about Amory Able. Wait and see!"

We all went tramping up to Dent Place in the snow. I kept a tight hold on Ronald's collar so that she wouldn't roll around and muss up her ribbon, but when we got to the Ables' house, she was so excited that she pulled away from me, dashed up the walk barking her head off, and flung herself against the door.

Unfortunately, someone was just opening the door, and Ronald accidentally knocked that someone down. It wasn't Amory Able or Maud either. Instead, it was a little girl.

"Down, Ronald!" I yelled, trying to grab hold of her collar again. "Sit! Lie down!"

Ronald paid no attention. She usually doesn't. She was licking the little girl's face, and the little girl was screaming.

"Don't be afraid!" I said. "She won't hurt you. She loves kids."

Then this strange woman ran up. She was about my mother's age but nowhere near as good looking. She had frizzy hair and buck teeth, and she started screaming too.

Ronald doesn't like grownups as much as she likes kids, so she got to barking again, and the place was like a madhouse until this familiar voice shouted over the rest of the noise.

"'Unbidden guests are often welcomest when they are gone.' Calvin Coolidge. TAKE THAT DOG HOME!"

As I dragged Ronald out the door, I could hear my father saying, "But that's Shakespeare!"

After I got Ronald home, I untied the red ribbon and threw it in the garbage, card and all. Then I gave Ronald a whole package of hot dogs, even though I knew I'd get in trouble for it.

"Merry Christmas!" I said. "This may be the last Christmas you ever have, so enjoy it!"

I cried all the way back to Dent Place.

"Merry Christmas, Martha dear!" said Maud when she opened the door. "We never had time for introductions, did we? I'd like you to meet my daughter Arabella."

I almost fainted. My father had to pull me indoors, and even then I didn't know what to say. To make things worse, I learned that the little girl Ronald knocked over was Arabella's daughter. She was five years old, and her name was Mary Lou. Mary Lou, not Martha.

Arabella's husband was there too. He was a skinny, shy-looking man, nowhere as good looking as my father. I asked if he was a dog trainer, and he said no, he was a stockbroker. I was beginning to feel pretty silly.

Well, my father stepped up and started to thank the Ables for letting me hang around so much all fall. "I hear my scamp of a daughter has adopted you as her second family!" he said. "I hope she isn't too much in the way."

"She has been our sunshine," said Amory Able solemnly.

" 'Sunshine,' I called her, and she brought, I vow,
    God's blessed sunshine to this life of mine.

"Robert Service," he said.

I thought that was pretty nice of him. It was the first time he had ever said anything complimentary, so I was a little disappointed when he added, "Ornery little thing, though. Wants to do everything her own way, regardless."

"We'll have to break her of that," said my father with a twinkle in his, and he quoted too:

". . . Woman in a bitter world must do the best she can—
Must yield the stroke, and bear the yoke, and serve the
    will of man . . .

"Robert Service."

"Ever hear of Women's Lib?" I asked him. "Besides, who taught you to quote Robert Service?"

"My eighth-grade English teacher," my father answered. "Against my will, let me tell you. Service is hardly my favorite poet!"

Things were getting worse and worse! I could tell that Maud thought so too because she took my father by the elbow and steered him into the dining room. But Amory Able followed right along, sputtering all this stuff about Robert Service.

"Only good poet this country ever had!" he kept saying. "Always kept his sense of humor, too. Robert Service is what this country needs right now, sir! He knew how to keep things under control. Did we have a problem with inflation back in those days? We did not! Did we have trouble in the Middle East? No, sir! And you could still buy a decent loaf of bread for only fourteen cents."

My father looked completely baffled. I was a little confused myself until it occurred to me that maybe Amory Able had gotten Robert Service mixed up with Calvin Coolidge. I tried to explain to my father, but I had a hard time getting it across. Anyway, my father wasn't really paying attention. He was looking at the food on the table.

Christmas dinner cooked by Maud was delicious. We had stuffed goose, which I thought existed only in books, and mince pie, which is good but a little weird. I got to sit next to Arabella, and I found out all about her life. It wasn't very exciting.

To begin with, Arabella wasn't there because she read my ad saying all was forgiven. She was there because she always comes home for Christmas. In fact, it turned out that she never ran away at all. She just got married and moved to California, which is all the Ables meant when they talked about her being gone. She was nice, but I had no regrets in passing her up as my real mother. In the first place, judging by those buck teeth, I'd be wearing braces. In the second place, it would mean that Mary Lou was my kid sister. Mary Lou was a real brat.

Amory Able sat on my other side. He insisted on eating his whole meal off the plate I made for him, even though I explained that it was meant for kippered herring. I told him he ought to keep it for special because I was afraid it might break.

Any normal person would have answered that Christmas *is* special, but not Amory Able. He snorted and said, " 'Sufficient onto the day is the evil thereof.' Calvin Coolidge."

Now, I knew perfectly well that came from the Bible because we had it once in church. But experience had taught me it was no use arguing with Amory Able, so I kept quiet.

Not my father, though. He swallowed a mouthful of mince pie and said, "Actually, I believe that's from the gospel according to Saint Matthew."

"Could be," said Amory Able. "But Calvin Coolidge said it first."

We didn't stay too long that afternoon because my father was really tired. He apologized to the Ables and explained about his long trip from South America and everything. But once we all had our coats on, he suddenly changed his mind.

"We have a Christmas tradition in our family," he told the Ables. "Why don't you join us? Let's all go to the zoo!"

Maud and Arabella weren't too enthusiastic, but Mary Lou started to cry when her mother said perhaps another time, so of course she got her own way.

We ended up in two cars: me with Amory and

Arabella's family, Maud with my parents and Kermit. My parents got there first because Amory Able drives about two miles an hour. He's the only person I ever knew who was stopped by the police for driving too slowly. He's also the only person I ever knew who didn't care. When the policeman told him to drive a little faster if he didn't want to cause an accident, Amory Able told him, " 'Haste makes waste!' Calvin Coolidge."

Well, when we got to the zoo, my parents had been waiting half an hour and Kermit was shivering, so my father made us race uphill from the parking lot. We raced all the way to the polar bears, and when we caught our breaths, we sang "Jingle Bells." The bears listened, but they weren't impressed.

The rest of the crowd arrived a few minutes later. They had been held up by Mary Lou, who refused to walk, so her father had to carry her. She was whining, and her nose was running. I wouldn't trade her for Kermit if you paid me a million dollars, so it's a good thing she's not my sister.

My father and Amory Able followed along behind, talking seriously. That is, Amory Able talked and my father had the serious look on his face that I happen to know means he's thinking about something else.

Amory Able was telling my father about the only proper way to raise a dog and why only a fool would write with washable ink and how to survive if you're lost in a blizzard.

My father nodded every time Amory Able said "Calvin Coolidge," right on cue.

"What shall we sing next?" my mother asked.

" 'Silent Night'!" Kermit and I shouted together.

But Mary Lou wanted to sing "Rudolf, the Red-nosed Reindeer," and when Kermit and I said it was too dumb, Mary Lou started crying again and wiped her nose on her mitten.

"It's my baby's favorite song!" said Arabella. "We wouldn't want to spoil her Christmas, would we?"

"Poppycock!" said Amory Able.

Then Arabella's husband-who-wasn't-a-dog-trainer said that Mary Lou looked cute as a picture when she sang "Rudolf, the Red-nosed Reindeer," and he wished he had his camera. I was gladder than ever that they weren't my real family.

Anyway, we sang, and some other people came by and sang too. Maud Able's voice warbled about two octaves over everyone else's, and she was completely out of tune. It didn't sound too good, but at least we were full of Christmas spirit.

All except Amory Able, I should say. He kept right on talking, even after my father stopped listening and started singing instead. No one was paying any attention to him, so he glared at the polar bears and told them why Coca Cola would curdle their guts and how to get a good sharp edge on a knife.

We switched to "Silent Night," and Amory Able switched to socks. "You'll find that if you're wearing two pairs of socks, you won't get blisters on your feet," he told the bears. "If you wear only one pair of socks, your shoes rub holes in your feet, but if you wear two pairs of socks, they rub against each other and leave your feet alone."

One of the bears yawned, and my father said it was getting late, so maybe we should skip the other animals and go home.

"I'll be along in a minute!" said Amory Able. "Got one more thing to say."

The rest of us turned back downhill. It was getting dark and cold, but it was beautiful. The street lamps came on all of a sudden, and the snow was all sparkly underneath. We could hear church bells from far away, which made where we were seem more quiet.

Then Amory Able must have finished what he had to say to the bears because I heard him shouting: "ONLY GOOD PRESIDENT THIS COUNTRY EVER HAD!"

It had been quite a day. I hardly had the energy to open my presents when we got home, and my father looked so tired that I was afraid he would spend the rest of his vacation in bed. But when I mentioned it, he said he hadn't had such an interesting Christmas in years and that Amory Able was a very unusual man.

"Did you get my letter?" I asked him when we were sitting in front of the fire that night. "Is that why you came home?"

"I'm afraid I didn't," said my father. "Don't worry, though. They'll forward it."

"But by the time it gets here, you'll be back in South America again!" I complained.

"No I won't," my father said. "I finished my work there earlier than I expected. Now I'm staying home. Better shine up your boots, Martha. Snow or no snow, we're going out to the farm next Sunday!"

My mother smiled. "I was dreading this Christmas, but it turned out to be the best one I can remember!"

"Me too. I bet we're the happiest family in the whole of Georgetown!" said Kermit.

As for me, I threw my arms around Ronald and burst into tears.

# Chapter 12

I wish I could say that everything was perfect from then on, that my father said, "Oh, Martha! Now that I know you care so much about Ronald, of course you can keep her forever!"

Instead, my father repeated what I had already heard a million times. We travel too much to have pets.

"But you just said you were staying home from now on!" I sobbed.

"The problem is that I can't be sure how long 'from now on' will last," my father explained. "Who knows? We may be sent somewhere in Europe next year. I've even heard talk about another post in East Africa."

That just made me feel worse, but then my father started talking really gently, so that I had to stop sobbing and listen. He told me how he loves dogs too and how he always had a dog when he was growing up, so he knew it was hard on me. Then he said that if I could find a family that would keep Ronald if we went away, he'd let Ronald stay with us for as long as we were in Georgetown.

Well, I gave up my idea of asking the Ables, but it struck me that I had forgotten to give a Christmas present to Parker, so I gave her forty-nine percent of Ronald Reagan. I didn't make it fifty because I wanted to have what my father calls the controlling share.

Parker was thrilled. She promised she would take care of Ronald if we went away, and she got her parents to agree. Only she didn't want to wait until we went away, so I had to let Ronald live in her house part of the time. That arrangement would have made me kind of unhappy if Parker weren't my best friend. But it worked out fine.

Another thing worked out fine too: Kermit and I never went back to Saint Michael's!

Not that my mother gave up her job. She said it agreed with her to work full time, but my father said that Kermit and I were old enough to come home from school and stay alone. So I wore the key on a string around my neck, and even when I went out to walk Ronald, I never, never forgot to lock the front door. At least, not more than once or twice.

One day the next spring Parker and I were walking Ronald together, and I told Parker the story about Arabella and the sailor who wasn't my father—who wasn't actually a sailor or even a dog trainer, but only a stockbroker.

"You mean you *wanted* to be an orphan?" Parker asked me. She looked really shocked.

I told Parker how I love my mother and father, but exciting things always happen to orphans in books, and it wouldn't hurt to have two sets of parents.

Parker shook her head. "You wouldn't like it. You'd

*hate* it!" she told me. "Believe me, it's awful to lie in bed in the middle of the night and wonder how some woman could have had you and then just given you away."

"It wouldn't happen like that," I started to tell her. Then I stopped. "You mean *you're* adopted?" I asked her.

"Yes," said Parker, "and I love my parents, the ones who adopted me. At least they really wanted me. If I ever met my true mother, I'd never forgive her! My parents keep saying I'm not supposed to feel that way, but I do."

"But you can't be sure!" I told her. "Maybe giving you up was the noblest thing your real parents ever did. Maybe they were just crazy about you, but there was some terrible danger to your life if they kept you—like Arab oil kings who wanted to kidnap you and hold you for ransom!"

"Fat chance!" said Parker.

"But listen, Parker!" I told her. "Your real parents might be anyone. Just *anyone*! Your father might have been President of the United States and you were born on the wrong side of the blanket."

"Which side is that?" asked Parker.

"It's something that happens in books," I said. "I think it means someone snatches you out of your mother's bed the very second that you're born."

Well, I could see it was no use arguing with her. She had some sort of psychological block against it, but there was nothing to stop me from solving the mystery on my own. It shouldn't be too hard after my experience with Arabella. I mean, now that I know all about birth certificates and advertising in the daily papers and all that. It might cost money, but you can't let a little thing like money get in your way when you're working for a noble cause.

Just suppose Parker's real mother had been Miss America and she eloped one day with the chief of police? It ought to be easy to track down a former Miss America. And when I found her, we'd have this big reunion with tears and everything, and Parker would be my best friend forever because she owed it all to me.

I decided to start with *The New York Times*.